CHOOSE YOUR OWN APOCALYPSE

A Collection of World-Ending Stories by

HOLLI ANDERSON   **D. J. BUTLER**   **ROBERT J DEFENDI**

JASON KING   **CRAIG NYBO**   **DANIEL SWENSON**

DAVID J. WEST   **JAMES WYMORE**

Edited by
JAMES WYMORE

Immortal Works LLC
P.O. Box 25492
Salt Lake City, Utah 84104
Tel: (385) 202-0116
www.immortal-works.com

Formatted by FireDrake Designs
www.firedrakedesigns.com

CONTENTS

INTRODUCTION

As I attended numerous panels and presentations at various conventions, I had two key thoughts. First, the people on the stage must be amazingly smart and talented so I should learn from their sage wisdom. Second, this feels like school and I wish it could be more interactive and fun. Lacking any real imagination of my own, I decided to copy a genius cartoon mouse and hatch a plan to take over the world through the power of fiction novels. First step: write a book. Second step: get on the panelist stand. Third step: rally the audience to riot and take control!

In retrospect, I should have come up with more steps.

Eventually I found an editor who liked my novels. Then I managed to get invited to be a panelist. However, no matter how many times I incited anger and frustration in the audience, they never rose up as planned. In a moment of rational contemplation, I realized that if I couldn't take over the world, I should probably end it.

In September of 2013, Salt Lake City held their first comic themed convention. (For legal purposes, let's call it FanX retroactively, to avoid the wrath of San Diego.) They asked the panelists to suggest panels. I knew my time had finally come. So, I pitched a panel that wasn't people talking but rather a full audience participation game that thinly veiled my plot to rally a rebellion. Again, to compensate for my lack of imagination, I borrowed a title from books I'd read as a kid. The panel name: CHOOSE YOUR OWN APOCALYPSE!

I started recruiting like-minded, disgruntled story tellers to "play" the game, with the understood and unspoken mutual goal of raising an army to bring destruction on the undeserving people of the world who refused to buy enough books to make me the unquestioned leader. And it worked, sort of. The audience rallied. Amidst laughter and cries of battle, we sorted them into groups that would later be given specific jobs in the new regime. But when it ended, the riot didn't spill over into the rest of the world.

Clearly, we needed a better strategy. Obviously, organization is my Achilles' heel. After several conventions with many audience members pledging their loyalty, I still didn't know how to turn that into an Armageddon.

After one of the best recruiting panels to date, at Westercon the next year, I had dinner with David J. West, R. A. Baxter, and D. J. Butler. There we realized a group of like-minded leaders would be more effective at disseminating the call to revolt. We invited Jason King to a super-secret meeting at a library, where nobody would suspect us of hatching such nefarious plans.

We contacted more devastation hungry allies, adding Holli Anderson, Craig Nybo, Robert J. Defendi, and eventually Daniel Swenson to our ranks. Each author determined to spread the word allegorically through novels and symbolically through game panels at numerous conventions. Soon I found myself wondering what I had done, when I saw their vigor for the cause begin even to outpace my own.

What you have before you is the latest in our unending efforts to herald the call to action. It is our sincerest desire that you will take some enjoyment while embracing the inevitable fate of the world, whatever form it finally takes.

-James Wymore

THEY ALL MUST DIE

Holli Anderson

I

The original home planet was a thing of the distant past —something that remained to them only in the memories injected into their cells as they formed in growth pods. The destruction of their planet could be blamed on no one but their own kind, their ancestors. Back then, they had been allowed to breed—and breed they did. They bred themselves right out of resources.

As the planet died, the smartest of the Entosadurians escaped on a fleet of interstellar ships they'd built but never tested. Those who'd built and knew how to run the ships put themselves in charge—after all, they were the most intelligent of those aboard. The first edict was to ensure that what had happened to their planet, didn't happen again. They only had enough sustenance to last twenty years, and that was only if they sustained their current population. So everyone was *voluntarily* sterilized via chemicals in the food. A secret level of the main ship contained the pods where any new Entosadurians would be genetically created by the scientist corps and left to gestate up to a certain point before being put into a state of hibernation. The gestation would continue after finding a new planet to call home.

They searched for a new home for twenty-one years. Desperation, as is usually the case, caused them to settle for something less than ideal. The new planet was an arid, barely habitable dung heap. They were survivors, though. And, they'd been surviving for millennia on the tiny planet they called Midden.

Chit had had enough. He convinced the leaders to send out a scouting party to try to find a more suitable home. They'd done much evolving since the original planet. They had many different versions of their original species. The big guys—the workers and the enforcers—stood sixteen feet or more. There hadn't been much need on Midden for them to enforce rules because of the genius of the founders—those that had made the decision to create all new life in the labs where they could inject into the DNA the inherent instinct to obey the most important of the laws. The smallest of the Entosadurians, the microscopic DNA extractors, made up the majority of the population because they were essential to its survival, took up almost no space, and used scant resources. Chit was one of the thinkers, the leaders of the planet. They ranged in size from that of a ladybug to a giant bird-eating spider.

Chit and his crew of five-hundred crash-landed on Earth after a ten-year search for a suitable planet. The first to exit the wreckage of the ship, Chit's stomachs flipped with disappointment. He surveyed his surroundings—this planet was even more undesirable than Midden. He detected very little water in the desolate environment surrounding them. The same terrain for as far as the eyes could see—and his dozens of eyes could see in every direction at once.

The early days were tough. Their ship was captured by a

group of humans wearing protective suits with special breathing apparatuses. What kind of planet had they landed on that the inhabitants had to use machines to breathe? Was Chit going to die from inhaling this air? He tested its makeup using his highly sensitive antennae. Nitrogen 78%, oxygen 21%, argon 1%, carbon dioxide .03%, plus a scant amount of water vapor and miniscule amounts of several other gasses. Perfect. The alien creatures on this planet must not have the same makeup as the Entosadurians.

The Earthlings took their ship along with six of the crewmembers that were unable to get out in time. Chit followed them as they loaded the ship into a hidden compartment buried under mounds of sandy dirt. He felt the vibrations of the earth beneath his six extremities as his ship descended into the depths below, relieved he'd been able to send a beacon to the leaders on Midden, guiding them here.

That had been decades ago—sometime in the 1950s in a place the humans called Area 51. Chit and his crew had since spread across the entire planet. They'd been relieved to find that only small portions of it had the inhospitable climate of their original landing site. The Entosadurians spread far and wide, from the Siberian taiga to the jungles of the Amazon and the uninhabited thermal valleys of the great southern continent—with the giant workers well hidden in the forests of Washington and Oregon in America. Chit laughed every time he heard of a Bigfoot sighting—boy did the humans have the wrong idea there! The rest of them hid in plain sight, blending in with the unintelligent insects that inhabited the planet.

Without the special chemicals being added to their food, his small crew of five-hundred started to reproduce again several years after their landing. There were now tens of billions of them on the planet Earth, communicating with each other by sending information from one tribe to another until it reached them all. They could transmit a message that would circle the globe in less than twelve hours.

Chit still led the group of overlooked aliens. Entosadurians lived long lives with the aging process leaving them virtually unaffected until well into their third century.

Surrounded by his highest ranking officers, Chit stood on the decaying fallen limb of one of the hundreds of trees surrounding them in the Uintah mountains. He paced back and forth on two of his appendages—like a human, only the size of a giant cockroach.

"It has been more than long enough for our entire wretched planet to make their way here. It's obvious they aren't coming. Maybe the transmission I sent right before the blasted humans found us didn't reach them. Who knows?" He stopped pacing, the clicks and clacks of the alien language fell silent for a moment as he looked out over the hundred officers. "It's time. Time to take over this planet before the soft-shelled, brain-fried humans destroy it. We can't wait any longer for reinforcements."

The clacking of dozens of chitinous mandibles could have been heard by even the massively inferior aural canals of the humans—had there been any close by. Chit allowed the officers their discussion for a couple of minutes before gaining their attention with a silent command sent via the genetic link they all shared. Thousands of eyes turned back to their commander.

"The time for discussion is past. The planning begins now."

"Sir." Flint, his closest friend and highest ranking officer, addressed him. "I submit that the first phase of the plan be the recovery of our ship and the Entosadurians taken by the humans. There were at least two workers in that group. Plus, if we have access to the ship we can try one last time to contact the home planet."

Chit dropped down on all six appendages as he thought. "Yes. Yes. I think that's a great idea. I'll lead the assault."

The plan was made and the officers disbanded to spread the word to the rest of their people. Chit walked with Flint away from any prying aural canals.

"Chit, you know that the chance that Ara is still alive is very slim. These barbaric humans probably killed her long ago. Dissected her like a lab animal." Flint's antennae flicked continuously, scanning his surroundings.

Clicking his mandibles together, Chit agreed. "I understand the odds. Yet, I feel strongly that we must try. I feel strongly that she lives. That she's been waiting for us."

"Your plan is solid. If she's there—if any of them are there and still alive—we will retrieve them. The humans won't even know we're there until it's far too late for them."

"Yes. We are the superior species and we will prevail. Go back to your brood, get some rest, lay with your mate. The war begins at dawn." Chit's chest filled with anticipation as he looked forward to the battle. Looked forward to taking this planet as his own at last. Looked forward to seeing Ara again...

———

The small battalion consisting of one hundred and fifty-thousand DNA extractors and five-thousand soldiers ranging in size from a couple of millimeters to several inches long, stood before their commander. The genetically modified hawks waited in formation as Chit addressed the assembled troops.

"Today we begin what we came here to do. There is no need for me to give a speech to motivate you, Entosadurian domination of this world has been our goal since our arrival decades ago. The hawks will take us to the Air Force base where we will board the cargo plane our intelligence has ensured is heading to our destination. Your team leaders know the plan and will fill you in once we're safely tucked away in the airplane. DNA team—you will head directly for the cockpit and position yourselves such that you can dispatch the pilots and take over the control from within the computer chips only if necessary. You are to stand down unless otherwise instructed. Soldiers are to enter with stealth and hide amongst the cargo.

"We do not—I repeat, *do not*—want to alert the humans of our presence. The success of this operation depends on the element of surprise at our final destination." Chit looked over his battalion, the group of microscopic DNA extractors visible only as a miniscule glowing dot to his specially attuned eyes. "Board your assigned hawk."

The troops fell out and mounted the waiting birds. The hawks, each genetically altered by the DNA extractors to obey the commands of the Entosadurians, took flight, soaring toward Hill Air Force Base.

———

"This is Angry Eagle requesting permission to enter Restricted Area 4808." The pilot flipped a few switches, entirely unaware that his plane had been invaded by an alien life form.

"Permission to enter 4808 Angry Eagle. The air strip is yours. Land at will."

Chit sent a series of commands to his troops in a pitch too high for the pilots and crew to register. "Ready alert. Prepare to disembark upon landing, prior to the opening of the cargo hatch." They would exit in the same manner they'd entered the jumbo jet, via small openings around the landing gear compartment.

"DNA-Es"—he pronounced this 'dannies'—"board your carrier soldiers now." The landing gear began to lower. He had to just assume they heard and obeyed the command. Unless they gathered in a large, close group, he couldn't see them without the use of a high magnification microscope.

The plane pulled sharply to the right as the wheels touched down, a strong gust of wind catching it broadside. The pilot wrangled the monstrous machine back in line with the air strip and hit the brakes hard before another gust could knock them off course. As they rolled to a stop, Chit slipped through a small crack and leaped to the ground, the wind pushing him sideways several yards before his extremities hit the ground and found purchase there, small hooks automatically erupting from his phalanges to keep him grounded.

The gusting wind hindered them but a small amount, thanks to their adaptable bodies, but it helped them immensely. Visibility, for the humans at least, was zero. The desert sand erupted around the advancing alien army, completely camouflaging them as they rushed toward the underground enclosure. Little had changed at the top secret base since the 1950s.

Pressure tightened around Chit's chest, not so much from anxiety over the impending war but from hope and anticipation at seeing his life-mate, Ara, again after all these decades. He forced his mind to concentrate on the mission. They had to get in first.

The dannies deployed from the backs of the soldiers who carried them as soon as the troops stopped at the concealed entrance leading underground. "Going in, sir," they communicated to Chit.

It took them mere seconds to infiltrate the alarm and access systems and override the computer programs. Chit didn't need their next transmission to let him know they'd succeeded, the sand shifted and an elevator rose from the ground before them.

"Override complete, sir," came the communication anyway.

"Great job, dannies." Chit then addressed the entire battalion. "We're in. Let's go!" He swallowed down the bile that rose from his stomachs and lurched forward. They wouldn't use the elevator, that would alert the humans to their presence. He hoped that when the humans investigated the breach of the elevator rising, they'd assume it had been caused by a computer glitch.

The aliens slithered down the elevator shaft at top speed, the clicking of their carapace the only sound. They spread out on all the levels with strict orders to report to Chit the second either the old ship or the imprisoned aliens were found.

Chit skittered all the way to the bottom floor—if the humans wanted to hide something, they'd hide it as deep down as they could. His best soldiers surrounding him, Chit turned down the lone hallway after exiting the elevator shaft. A not so subtle slant to the tiled floor took them further into the depths beneath the desert. Chit's group had their own contingent of DNA-Es with them, carried on the back of one of the soldiers. The overhead lights flickered.

"Prepare to switch to echolocation navigation," Chit said.

Another contingent must have encountered the enemy and put the next step of the plan into play—shutting down the entire electrical system, starting with the lights. The DNA-Es made quick work of their assignment. The lights shut down with a whir and a click, plunging the corridor into complete darkness. Even the highly attuned visual receptors in the optics of the aliens could make nothing out in the sheer blackness surrounding them. They had other options, however... many other options—unlike their foes, the humans, who relied much too heavily on their vision.

A startled yelp came from down the hallway, behind a locked door. "That's our target," Chit said. "Move forward."

No need for stealth now that the enemy was engaged, Chit began the war cry—the high pitched warbling chitter that struck primal fear into all other beings, especially humans. He and his contingent blasted down the hallway, the carrier soldiers in the lead. The DNA-Es entered the electrical lock, and the door sprung open as they overrode the computer commands. Within seconds, the other doors in the black corridor sprung open as the DNA-E detachment tasked with shutting everything down, completed their assignment. Chit nodded, clenching his mandibles in satisfaction at the flawless work of his littlest soldiers.

Chit made for one of the five humans inhabiting the room. He leaped and grasped onto the human's clothing, scrambling up to its shoulder. He plunged his right, front appendage into the human's carotid artery, sensing the warm pumping of blood before he'd even completed his rapid climb up the person's torso. The transfer of the specialized toxin they'd used on their enemies for millennia occurred before the human brain even processed the sting of the puncture. With a slight jerk of its hand—probably just receiving the message from its brain to swipe at the foreign object in its neck—the human fell dead to the floor.

Chit felt the warmth in his thorax as the toxin replenished itself within the special pouch that grew inside all the Entosadurian soldiers.

"Battalion check in," he communicated.

All contingents responded—every human within the building had been dispatched.

"Band numbers ten, six, and thirteen secure the perimeter. Kill all humans within one-half mile of this outpost, and then stand guard." Chit jumped to the top of a metal table. "Dannies, lights!"

The Entosadurians' eyes needed no adjustment period—the Elders had thought of everything when enhancing their DNA. The five humans lay sprawled on the floor; all adorned in white lab coats.

A familiar voice he hadn't heard in decades permeated Chit's aural canals. Bindu, a female worker/enforcer that had been on the original transport that crash landed there in the desert hell, said, "Chit? Is that you?"

"Bindu? Yes! Yes, it's me! Where are you?"

"Bottom level. I'm in the cell marked 'Living Specimens' just off the main corridor."

"We're on our way."

His onyx-colored blood pumped faster through his system —if Bindu survived, maybe Ara did, too. He hurried down the now-lit corridor, his band of soldiers following. He looked up at the doors as he ran, searching for the right one.

"Living Specimens," he said as they reached it. "Dannies, get us in." The door had an electronic scanner attached to the side. The DNA-Es made quick work of it, the inner workings of the metal door clanged just before it whooshed open. "Bindu?"

Chit climbed up the wall to greet his old shipmate at the level of her face—fifteen feet in human measurements, she was short for a worker. "Bindu, it's so good to see you!"

"It's good to see you, too, Chit." Her body—covered in long, spider-like hairs—quivered. "What took you so long?"

Chit looked down. What had taken him so long? Fear of finding them all long dead? Fear of capture? "I don't have a good answer for that, other than we needed time to build up our army. We couldn't strike here until we had the capability to strike everywhere."

"And... we now have that capability?" she asked.

"Yes. This is the first battle of the war to take over this planet. Finally." Chit's antennae rotated 360 degrees and back. "Bindu... where's... where's Ara. And the rest of the crew?"

Bindu lowered her head, her ape-like forearms drooped at her sides. "I should show you. Follow me."

Chit's stomachs dropped. This wasn't a good sign. He followed the worker around a corner inside her large cell to another door. A door labeled "Dissection Room".

"Dannies..." he said through clenched mandibles.

The door whooshed open and Bindu stepped aside to allow Chit to enter. His antennae retracted immediately. The stench! The odor of death made his stomachs churn, bile pumping backward up his throat. With frantic movements of his dozens of eyes, he searched the room in every direction at once. Then, all eyes focused in one spot on the back wall.

Chit's abdominal wall contracted, and his stomachs' contents projected out between his mandibles in a powerful stream, hitting the wall with a hiss as the acid burned through the paint.

"No! Ara. Oh, what have they done to you!" Framed like a work of art in a horror museum, his life-mate's body hung sliced open and pinned to a canvas behind the glass, her organs removed from the open cavity and strewn out next to her. "Beasts! Why would they..." he spun to face Bindu, his six-inch height suddenly seeming big enough to fill the room. "Why did you allow this?"

"Chit," she hung her humongous head. "I failed you. I failed them all. They separated and secluded us immediately upon arrival. They did this"—she swept her hands to indicate the carnage hanging from the walls—"to everyone but me. I don't know why they chose to preserve my life, other than the President wanted to keep one of us alive. All in the name of science."

Staring at the displayed remains of his loved-one, his

antennae popped out again, followed by barbed spikes that erupted all along his carapace and limbs. His eyes spun in all directions as he commanded, "Kill. Them. All."

The original plan had been to only kill the humans who opposed them in battle. Chit straightened to his full 6.3 inches and commanded again, "Kill them all. Every last one of them. Kill them, and eat their demonic carcasses. Spread the word. The war starts now."

II

"Chit, wait..." Flint protested.

"That's Commander Chit, Officer." Chit stood at the front of the assembled group of officers. They'd called an emergency meeting after Chit's directive to kill all of the humans had reached every quarter. "I've made up my mind. They all need to die."

"Commander," Flint stood taller, "that isn't the plan we agreed on."

The officers stood in the "Dissection Room", most of their eyes averted away from the wall hangings of their crew-mates and friends. Chit had insisted the meeting be held there—where they couldn't ignore the demented murders the humans had committed. The depraved and heartless inhabitants of this planet who had no concern for anyone but their own kind. Sometimes, often times, not even their own kind.

"They do not deserve to live." Chit leaned in toward his officers. "Look around you. Does this look like the work of someone we should show mercy to? They showed no mercy to Ara or the others." He stood straight again, and focused on Ara's dissected and splayed body. "We will show them no mercy."

"Commander," Bindu stepped in front of Ara's framed

remains, blocking Chit's view. "They aren't all like that. They aren't all bad."

"Hmf." Chit grunted. "You've lived among them too long. They've brainwashed you into believing they have worth."

"The only worth the humans have is to be used as fodder for our children and as fertilizer for the soil," Sen, a female officer, spat. Her brother's remains hung just below and to the right of Ara's.

Bindu sighed. "No. They are not all the same. Some of them have good hearts."

"Which ones, Bindu?" Chit asked. "The children who pull the legs off grasshoppers and set them in ant piles? Or, the teens who use drugs and riot and set fire to buildings? Maybe it's the grown men and women who start wars, kill animals for fun, or burn down forests?"

"Some of them are good," Bindu repeated. "The doctors, nurses, and medics who save, the police and soldiers who protect, the mothers who teach their children to respect life. Some of them are good."

"Bah!" Chit yelled. "I don't even know why I allowed you in here, you need to be deprogrammed." He turned to his own battalion of soldiers. "Sergeant, take her to another room. Dannies, send a contingent with them, and begin deprogramming immediately."

"Chit," Bindu said in a dangerously quiet voice. "I do not need to be deprogrammed. I am not brainwashed. And... I will not leave this room."

Chit stared at her, chest rising with each deep breath. "I could easily have you killed for insubordination, Captain. Your size seems to make you think you have an advantage over your smaller peers—something learned from the humans, I'm sure. 'Size is power!' 'Might makes right!' 'Only the strong survive!'" He spat acidic bile onto the floor. "But... you're wrong. As are they. The tiniest of our kind can kill you in an instant. You wouldn't even know it was happening. Remember, Bindu?"

"Yes, Commander, I remember. Kill me if you must, I will not fight any of you. But, please, hear me out first."

"Maybe it is you, my friend," Flint said quietly, "who needs to be reprogrammed. It is the edge of insanity to insist we stay in this room full of corpses. You've always taken the time to listen to us before. Why not now?" He took his friend by the upper limb with a gentle touch. "Let us move from this room of horrors so we can have this discussion within an environment not wrought with grief and pain."

Chit jerked his appendage away from Flint and looked at his friend. "Fine. We'll move to the wreckage of the ship. We need to try to send another message back to Midden anyway." He glanced toward Bindu. "Lead us, Captain. Move out."

———

"So, Flint," Chit slumped down into the pilot's seat of their long-downed spaceship, "what do you propose we do from here, if not complete annihilation?" He slammed his clawed fist down on the emergency transmit button—the one that would send a message to their long-term, temporary home planet, Midden, along with coordinates to reach Earth.

Flint stood to address the assembled officers. "I propose that we hit hard and fast, kill millions all over the world in a concerted strike that takes less than an hour. This will show the humans our superior might, and those who remain will submit to our rule for fear of annihilation." He paused. "We hit the military and law enforcement agencies in this first— and hopefully only—strike."

Not looking at his friend, Chit said, "And, what do we do with the humans we allow to survive?"

"We move them to a central location where we can keep

constant surveillance on them. Maybe in a desert somewhere where they will become completely dependent on us for their day-to-day survival. That can all be worked out after the initial strike. After all nations have surrendered to the Entosadurians." Finished, Flint returned to his ranks in the crowd.

Chit jumped from his seat, and started pacing on his bottom four limbs. Flint was probably right. It was almost the exact plan they'd agreed to in the beginning. His own plan. But... his mind returned to the glassed in frame on the Dissection Room wall. His love. His Ara. Sliced open and splayed out for humans to study and gloat over. Pinned to a board like a common insect. "Bindu," he said. "Tell me specific reasons you believe humans are worth sparing."

"Sir," she said, standing. "Throughout my years of captivity I have been shown kindness by many humans—even up to colluding with me in a botched escape attempt. I've had long conversations with them and understand that they are most definitely not all of one mind. Their thoughts and ideas, convictions and beliefs, range far and wide. Some are dead-set that they're in the right and will employ no discourse with anyone who disagrees—these are the dangerous ones, no matter what their ideals. But most, in my experience, are open to discussion and ideas different than their own. They care about life—not just human life, but all life.

"One scientist in particular was appalled and disgusted at what was done to the Entosadurians in the Dissection Room. She wept bitter tears as she apologized to me for what her peers had done." Bindu stood in front of Chit. "There are many such instances of good humans, Commander. I agree with Flint's plan only reluctantly and with sadness, knowing that a great show of force is indeed necessary to demonstrate to them that fighting back is futile. They have fighting spirits, these humans, and anything short of complete domination will only bring out the fighter in them."

Silence enveloped the crowded cockpit. Chit knew he could only carry out his plan with the cooperation of the others. Fine. He'd give Flint's strategy a chance... and if it failed... *when* it failed—his plan would be their only recourse. He stood at his full height, clapping his appendages down to his sides. "We will proceed with Flint's plan. Immediately. Go, now, and spread the word. The attacks will begin in three hours all over the planet."

———

The first wave of attacks was a complete success for the Entosadurians—and a devastating loss for the humans of Earth. The military and law enforcement officials of the world were caught completely off guard by an enemy they didn't even know existed until the killing started. From the highest commanders to the lowliest foot soldiers, the annihilation was complete in less than an hour.

As world leaders scrambled to make sense of the slaughter and form a defense against the nearly invisible and unknown foe, Chit decided the best course of action would be to destroy them, too, placing the world in even more chaos as those who ran the governments dropped to the ground, dead, within three hours following the death of the military. For the arrogant humans, it was a reign of terror unlike anything they'd ever imagined. All carried out seemingly from nowhere by, what they thought at first, a bunch of insects.

"We missed some important targets." Chit, along with his local officers, met at their newly designated headquarters at Area 51. They had to replenish their systems in order to produce more of the toxin used by the soldier forces. "The POTUS was able to escape to Air Force One before our

Washington contingency reached the White House. They are keeping her in the air by using a refueling jet. All other air traffic has been grounded. I'm not too concerned about this, we'll be able to reach her soon enough—we already have troops on the ground to intercept the refueling jet upon its next landing."

"What other targets were missed?" Flint asked.

"Everyone that's out on the oceans. Naval ships mostly."

Silence greeted the group of assembled leaders. The one thing the Entosadurians had been unable to create an adaptation for since their arrival on Earth, was seawater. Even just thirty seconds of exposure to the salinized liquid and they—all forms of them—bloated to an unrecognizable blob before disintegrating into a smudge of sticky goo.

"Gah!" Flint growled. "Why does this blasted planet have to have sodium chloride in its vast oceans! Any ideas for how to reach them out there?"

"Sir," Sen raised an appendage. "They will have to return to land eventually, to refuel and resupply. They aren't indefinitely self-sustaining – especially when it comes to food. I say, we just wait them out."

Chit clamped his mandibles together with a snap. "That will have to be the plan for now. But continue to study this. There has to be a way to reach them, even with all the planes grounded. The hawks can't fly out that far..." He shook his head, thinking.

"Sir," Bindu said. "Could we commandeer a ship and reach them that way?"

"I've thought about that. As deep out into the ocean as they are, it would need to be a very large and seaworthy ship... We would need to study the workings of such a machine. That will be our Plan B if they take too long to come to shore. I think we will be better off waiting, for now."

"When do we begin the second phase of our plan?" Flint asked. "The gathering of the remaining humans?"

"We must do it in waves." Chit tapped a clawed appendage on the control panel. "The first wave must go to build the shelters and other necessary infrastructure. The New Elders have suggested we split them up so there is one camp on each continent. They have already chosen desert locations on each one." He waved his claw in the air. "That isn't our concern, however. We will send a contingent of soldiers, and some worker/enforcers to each location to keep order. The rest is up to the New Elders to plan."

———

The rich and powerful humans grabbed all the scientists they could round up, and went into hiding. They thought their underground bunkers—built with just such an apocalypse in mind—would be safe. How could anyone—or anything—penetrate the three-foot thick cement walls, the extravagant alarm systems, the layers of defense? They'd expected the end to come at the hands of the strong: bombs, air raids, nuclear attacks, human soldiers with big weapons... *climate change*.

In their arrogance, the humans never even dreamed that their demise would come at the hands—or appendages—of intelligent microscopic beings and their larger counterparts. It was a simple matter for the Entosadurians to find them. Their senses were so fine-tuned that they could feel the vibrations in the earth above even the deepest of bunkers. It was easy from there to send in the DNA-Es to wreak havoc with the defense systems and open the bunkers wide. They got them all... or so Chit and his leaders thought.

As the aliens gathered up the masses, most went willingly. Especially in those areas of the earth where they were used to authoritarian leadership. Out with the old and in with the new, it made no difference to them who demanded their obedience—they followed the Entosadurians like the good little puppets they'd been groomed to be. The biggest problems came from North America, the United States in particular. The red states in particular. Those who had been raised to believe they were "free". Flag-waving, gun-toting survivalists.

Chit lost more than a few good soldiers to the redneck nation. They were strong and cunning, unlike they'd been portrayed in human movies and other media. Rounding them up turned out to be quite difficult, and, although Chit admired their tenacity and strength, he ended up commanding his troops to exterminate any humans who didn't obey with the relocation order immediately. He refused to lose any more soldiers.

During his decades on Earth, Chit had seen the humans as mostly buffoons, especially their political leaders. It didn't matter the nation, he saw the leaders as puffed-up, lying, gold-digging narcissists who only had their own best interests at heart. In the forest area that he called home on this planet, he'd come in contact with very few humans—and those he had observed close up seemed simple-minded at best. He shook his head as he thought about the twice weekly reports he'd received all these years from his intelligence agents out living among them. Buffoons. The lot of them.

"I think I'll go with the area Round-up Contingent tonight," Chit said to Flint at their morning briefing. "Our desert facility is ready for occupants, and I'd like to help bring in the first load."

"Do you think that's wise?" Flint leaned back, resting his carapace on the defunct control panel of their crashed spaceship. "The humans out this way are not likely to come without a fight."

"That's why I want to join them. I don't want there to be

any hesitancy in our troops when it comes to dispatching the uncooperative. We need to set the tone of no tolerance right at the beginning of this transport... we don't want to have the same issues we ran into in Australia."

"I understand." Flint pushed himself to a standing position. "I'll go with you, then."

Chit nodded.

———

Just over a million Entosadurian soldiers, with another million DNA-Es riding on a few of their backs, set out at a quick pace, Chit in the lead. They hit the rural areas of the southwest United States first—and the humans there were ready for them. Even though Chit had ordered the destruction of all TV and cell communications, these westerners had other ways of knowing what was going on in other parts of the world. Chit hadn't prepared for—or even known about—the extensive HAM radio operators throughout the world. These humans knew about the gatherings that had taken place in other countries.

Chit should have had some clue when his contingent reached the small town of Alamo, Nevada and had to scramble around, through, and over the quickly constructed barriers that surrounded it. The barriers—thrown together with chunks of broken cement and asphalt, chopped up desks and other furniture, trees, and whatever else they'd found to add to the pile—had wide openings compared to the small invaders. The large worker/enforcers climbed over without any issues. Chit laughed at the feeble attempt—until his heightened senses caught sight of a sentry positioned atop a wooden tower. The sentry wore night vision goggles and held a hand-held radio close to his mouth. Chit heard the click as the human depressed the button and said, "They're here."

With a series of loud clacks, Chit ordered a small contingent to take the man out. As the soldiers climbed the tower, the man pulled the pin on a grenade and lobbed it into the section of barriers nearest him. Chit scoffed, knowing his troops had already passed through the wall of detritus. The grenade exploded, setting off a series of explosives that must have been buried in the ground beneath the wall. He scuttled to hide under an abandoned truck as his aural canals pulsed with the screams of his soldiers.

Chunks of cement and furniture rained down on them, cracking their armor-like carapaces and crushing many of them.

"Go, go, go!" Chit yelled. "Kill any of them who do not immediately surrender!" He looked around for Flint, frantic to find his friend. "Flint! Report!"

He breathed a sigh of relief as his friend's distinctive clicks reached his ears.

"I'm okay. Leading my section into the town."

The Entosadurians injected toxin into nearly all of the residents of Alamo. It was a feisty town, with most residents unwilling to go peacefully. As the morning sun threatened to peak over the horizon in the east, Chit and his remaining soldiers escorted a small group of humans consisting of three men, six women, and twenty small children, out of town and into the surrounding desert.

Chit fell back to walk next to the humans, fuming with anger at the loss of hundreds of his soldiers.

A human child, female by the looks of her, looked down at him as he walked beside her light-up shoes, flashing in the dawning light of day as she stepped. "Where aw we going?" She asked with a sniffle.

Chit glared up at her. He figured her to be around four years old—humans developed *so* slowly compared to other species. Entosadurians were fully grown and developed six weeks after hatching. "To your new home." He answered her in her own language. Another thing that didn't make any sense to him. Why did the humans use so many different languages? Maybe they wouldn't have been so easy to conquer if they all understood each other like the Entosadurians did.

"Is it a vewy long walk?"

"No," Chit answered, curtly.

"I like bugs." The girl jogged a few steps to catch up to him as he tried to move away from her. "What kinda bug aw you?"

"We aren't *bugs*, little human child. We are Entosadurians. Aliens from another planet." He walked faster.

"You look like bugs," the little girl said with innocence.

"And that's why it was so easy to infiltrate your planet. You humans give no heed to those you deem smaller and weaker than yourselves." Why was he talking to this child when all he really wanted to do was execute his original plan and kill them all?

"You awen't weak. You'we shells are vewy hawd—hawdew than a snail's!"

Chit stopped and stared back at the snot-nosed child. "Do you know this because you've smashed snails before? Do you *like* bugs, or do you like to *kill* and torture bugs?"

She caught up to him and crouched down, squinting at him. "No! I don't kill 'em. I watch 'em." She dropped her gaze for a second before looking back at him. "I did accidently squish a roly-poly once when I was playing with my dog. I cwied fow a long time."

The sadness in her eyes made Chit pause. Was this human child telling the truth? Did some of them actually have feelings for something different than themselves? He shook his head and started walking again.

"What's you name?" the girl asked.

"Chit. What's yours?" Why did he ask that? He didn't care!

"Ohh! Chit is a awesome name!" She kicked up dirt as she caught up to him again. "My name is Hailey."

"Well... Hailey. I have to go to the front of the troops, now. Don't follow me." He scrambled away from the girl, his conflicting emotions swirling around inside of him. She had to be a spy. A plant. Humans didn't have feelings for bugs. His mind flipped back to Ara's dead body on display in the humans' lab. Bindu's words infiltrated his attempt to discount this child's claims, *some of them are good.* He shook his head. *No.* They'd killed hundreds of his soldiers this day. No, they weren't good. He wouldn't disrespect his dead soldiers—or his dead mate—by allowing himself to be fooled by a little girl.

———

As the soldiers that had been dispatched to the states farther away began to return with their groups of humans, the desert compound filled up. The humans were separated into work groups and given tasks they were required to perform each day before receiving food. Water was supplied to them as needed... so the weak species didn't die of dehydration in the desert heat. After the disaster in Alamo, Nevada, Chit sent out a directive to send the DNA-Es in first to find and destroy hand held or CB radios. While they did that, the small munitions force (all the size of ants) found and disarmed any and all explosives and removed the firing pins from all guns—even those that were in the hands or holsters of the humans.

Chit, against all reason and as hard as he tried to resist the urge, found himself more and more often visiting the human compound. Visiting the girl, Hailey, in particular. She had been assigned, along with the other younger children, to clear the planting area of rocks. Her hands had been worked raw the first couple of weeks, but she rarely complained. In fact, she thanked Chit for assigning her to rock duty, explaining, "I get to see all kinds of bugs when I pick up the wocks!"

She'd been reprimanded multiple times by the enforcers for stopping to watch a centipede scurry away or to inspect a group of ants as they built their dirt mound fortresses. Chit, against everything he'd commanded the enforcers to do with the humans, pulled Bindu aside and asked her to talk to the others about taking it easy on the four-year-old girl and her fascination with insects. He observed her as she stepped so carefully so as not to harm so much as a termite with her flashing shoes.

"Chit?" Hailey sat on the hard ground, her face red from the heat, as she took a drink break with the other kids in her group. "Why don't we have any books hewe? Or school? I should be leawning stuff."

He'd purposefully refused to let the humans bring books —or anything really—and hadn't allowed them to have any sort of formal schooling set up in their new compounds. They were unnatural, horrible beasts and only used education and learning to destroy each other. He didn't really understand the need for formal education, anyway. The Entosadurians didn't need to be educated, they were hatched with all the knowledge they'd ever need imbedded into their DNA. It was a much more efficient method than the years of *school* the humans attended.

"You will learn everything you need to know by working in the compound," he answered.

"I won't leawn how to wead..." Her mouth turned down in a frown.

"You don't need to."

"But... I *want* to." Her tiny voice quivered.

"Bah," Chit said. "It isn't necessary."

"Maybe for my biwthday, I can get a book?" She looked at him with hope shining in her big, blue eyes.

"We... we don't celebrate the day of your birth, here, Hailey. It's just another day." His traitor heart fluttered as her eyes filled with tears. "But... maybe. Just this once."

Hailey's eyes brightened.

"When *is* your birthday?" Chit asked, cursing himself for caring.

"August 4th!" She smiled. "And it's a special biwthday 'cause I'll be five and five means I can go to..." Her voice dropped to a near whisper. "...kindewgawten."

Chit couldn't take the disappointment in her face any longer. He didn't want her to influence him anymore. He still tried to hold to the belief that she was some sort of spy. "I have to go. Get back to work."

———

"So, Bindu," Chit said quietly. "This conversation stays between you and me. Got it?"

"Of course."

"When you said that some humans were good... did you really mean that?"

"Yes," Bindu answered. "I did. I do."

"I..." He bent backwards, cracking his vertebrae. "If you're right... and I'm not convinced that you are... but, if you are... what is your recommendation as to the future of the surviving humans?"

"I am honored that you asked my opinion, Commander." She took a deep breath. "I would let them go back to their homes—with close Entosadurian supervision, of course. Those that submit to our rule, can lead semi-normal, happy lives. Those who don't submit..." She shrugged.

He nodded. "Thank you for your honest thoughts. I'm

certainly not ready to give them that much freedom at this point. But... that may be an option in the future." Chit looked down at the tiled floor. "Now, do you have any idea where I can get a book for a child. Maybe a book about... insects."

Bindu hid her smile. "Yes, sir. I think I can take care of that for you. When would you be wanting this book?"

"By August 4th." He looked up. "And, Bindu... remember, this is between us."

———

Bindu carried the book, following a nervous Chit into the human compound. He walked straight to the field he knew Hailey would be working in that day and as soon as he spotted her, he picked up his step.

"Hailey, come sit with me for a minute," he said.

"Okay, Chit." She tossed the rock she held onto the pile.

"Do you know what day it is today?" Chit asked as she sat on the ground in front of him.

She shook her head with a frown.

"It's August 4th..."

"My biwthday..." she whispered. She looked up from where she'd been staring at her lap. "I'm five."

"Yes. And... I... umm... I got you something." He waved toward Bindu and she leaned down and handed the children's picture book on insects to the little girl.

"A book!" she squealed, hugging the book to her chest. "A book about bugs! Oh, Chit, I love you! Thank you! Thank you so much!"

Chit couldn't hide his smile. Some of the other children stopped what they were doing and stared in their direction. Chit cleared his throat and adopted a serious tone. "Now, back to work, human. You can look at the book on your own time."

"May I go put it undew my bed in the bunkhouse, please?" Her eyes sparkled.

"Yes, but then straight back to work."

Hailey blew him a kiss and started to skip toward the bunkhouse with her book held tight to her chest. She stopped and turned back to look at him. "Can you come see me tonight? We can look at it togethew."

Chit swallowed the lump in his throat. Unaccustomed emotions surfaced and it took a moment for him to get control of them. "Maybe. I'm a busy commander, Hailey. But... maybe I'll stop by tonight." He would stop by. There was something about her smile and the way her adorable eyes sparkled that made him... happy. Yes, he would stop by later.

———

"Commander!" one of the sentries called out.

"Yes, soldier? What is it?" Chit asked.

"Captain Flint requests your presence at headquarters ASAP, sir."

"On my way."

He clicked out a tune to a song Hailey had taught him as he headed toward the wreckage of their old spaceship. He entered the bay where they'd set up headquarters. "Flint? What did you need?"

"Ah, Chit! I have great news." The nervousness in Flint's voice made Chit wonder if he believed his own words.

"Well..." Chit gestured for his friend to continue.

"We've received word from Midden. The others... all of them... they'll be here tonight."

"Tonight?" Chit's stomachs churned with acid. "But...

that's impossible. Even with our fastest ships, it should take them years to reach Earth."

"They actually did receive the first transmission we sent when we arrived on this planet. They spent several of the last decades building ships and convincing everyone that it was time to abandon Midden. They've been traveling for the last eight years, lost the last couple. When we sent the new transmission, they were able to lock on to it. They were close-by; they just didn't know it."

"Okay... good." Was it good? Chit worried that the old Elders would try to take over command. He'd been in charge too long to just give up control. What if they wanted to revert back to the old ways he and his new Elders and officers had long abandoned? Well, the reinforcements would be good. They could now take care of the Navies that had been avoiding them out in the oceans. "Good job, Flint. We'll prepare to greet them with a large welcome upon landing."

––––––––

All available troops stood in formation beside the enormous landing zone. Chit and many of his officers, including Flint, waited atop a guard tower for the arrival of the rest of the Entosadurians from the planet Midden.

Since their attack on humans had begun weeks prior, air traffic had been all but shut down. An occasional human pilot in small, rural airports, had been able to sneak past the ranks of Entosadurians and take to the sky. Of course, it did little good, since as soon as they landed, they were... taken care of. The clear, blue sky stretched for miles without a cloud or airplane in sight. Chit heard the approaching spaceships before he spotted them. Feelings of nostalgia flooded over him as the once familiar sound of their engines, unlike anything the humans had, pounded the airwaves around him.

He searched the skies until a dot appeared in the distance. Then another. And another. A total of twelve ships approached and landed within ten minutes of his first sighting. Chit began to descend the tower in order to greet the newcomers.

"Hail Commander Chit!" A voice he recognized as Delta, the head and oldest Elder, sounded above the cooling of the engines. "Stay there, we'll come to you!"

Chit stood stiffly as his former leaders ascended the tower. He relaxed inside a fraction when Delta greeted him with the formal acknowledgement of an equal. Good. That meant they weren't planning on usurping his command... yet.

"Commander," Delta nodded. "It's good to see you. You've accomplished a great deal since you left us."

"It's good to see you as well, Elder Delta."

Delta surveyed the surrounding terrain, able to see for miles from the vantage point of the tower. "This is... seems to be... quite barren land. Not much better than Midden."

"That's exactly what we thought when first landing here, Elder." Chit looked toward the western horizon. "This planet is vast, however. With as many different terrains as one can imagine. We Entosadurians have spread to every continent and now rule the entire planet. It will be much easier to explore and visit the other areas now that we have air transportation."

"Just how vast is..."

The low rumble of a large jet engine in the distance cut him off. Chit looked at Delta. "That isn't one of ours, is it." It wasn't a question. He already knew the answer.

"What..." Delta and the other Elders looked at Chit. "Is that *yours*?"

"No. No, we don't fly the human's planes. They're too dependent on hydraulics and mechanics instead of computers. Too hard for us to manipulate the controls." He watched as a gigantic 747 came into view, followed by several smaller planes and two helicopters.

"Take cover!" he yelled out to the troops and the new arrivals. His troops ran toward the underground buildings, half of the new arrivals followed them, the other half scurried for the spaceships they'd just disembarked from. Chit's optics focused on the large, low-flying plane. His mandibles clamped shut so hard his carapace felt like it would crack as he recognized the 747 for what it was... an air tanker. A *super* air tanker. He'd seen them used to help put out forest fires. What were they hauling? Too late, his frantic thoughts landed on a horrible understanding of what might be inside those enormous tanks. "No..." Before he could warn those on the ground, the hatches on the bottom of the tanker opened up, right above the human compound. Seawater—tens of thousands of gallons of it—dumped onto the humans and Entosadurians on the ground. The smaller planes and helicopters dumped their loads in the areas that didn't get soaked by the 747.

"Hailey!" Ashamed that thoughts of the human girl invaded his mind at a time when his entire command was under attack, he yelled to the Elders and officers, "Inside, get inside the tower!" He ushered them in before following behind them. The 747's engines roared as it rose in the air, belly now empty.

The desert sand soaked up the deluge of murderous seawater but not fast enough to save those who'd been on the ground during the onslaught. The underground buildings had been built to be water-tight in the case of a heavy rain—not so much for having an ocean dumped on the porous ground above. The Entosadurians who had taken shelter belowground were swamped. Most of them died a writhing, miserable death within minutes of the attack.

Staring down at the bloating carcasses of his people,

Chit's mind kept wandering to the little human girl he'd reluctantly grown fond of. *It's her birthday. We were supposed to look at her book together tonight. Maybe she survived...* Anger flared inside him like a red-hot poker. Anger at himself for losing control of his thoughts. Anger at Hailey for tricking him into having feelings for her. Anger at the humans who had somehow figured out their weakness—and found a way to use it against them.

"Flint!" Chit yelled. "Send a message out. We need everyone to report in. Maybe we were the only ones to get hit." He turned to Bindu. "Take me to inspect the compound."

The worker/enforcers, like Bindu, had wrapped their feet in tarp material and gone out to look for any survivors and gather up the bodies of the millions of dead. Bindu carried him on her shoulder.

"Go to the field."

She nodded. She knew where he wanted to go, he was sure —she'd been with him that morning to deliver the book.

Many of the humans had survived, the seawater not toxic to their bodies. But many had drowned in the initial deluge or been swept into buildings or rocks or crevasses, their bodies smashed and mangled.

"I'm sorry, Commander," Bindu whispered as she came to a stop in front of a tree.

There, hanging from a lower branch, was the body of the little human girl. Hailey.

———

Reports came in from all over the world. Most of the Entosadurians were safe. The rebels only hit certain countries—countries where the big air tankers were available and coastal areas where they could easily pump water directly from the sea. Intelligence—too little, too late—reported that a large group of the rich and powerful had grabbed up a bunch of scientists and retreated out to sea on a moderate-sized cruise ship, nabbing a few "specimens" on their way. They tested their Entosadurian "specimens" with all sorts of chemicals, radiation, poisons—and came up empty on a way to kill the resilient alien species. The discovery of the aliens' weakness came by accident when one of the "specimens" fell into a bucket of mop water pulled from the sea so as not to waste the fresh water supply. After testing the seawater on the remaining aliens, the humans quickly formed and executed their plan—a plan they dubbed "Noah's Ark".

Chit had gained control of his emotions and now stood in front of the surviving Entosadurians at Area 51, his speech being spread out to all the earth as he gave it.

"Humans are a despicable species. We gave them a chance to survive and be taken care of under our rule—and they showed they can't be trusted. Humans showed, with this act of war as with many others in their short history, that they have no respect for life—not even, or maybe especially, the lives of their own people. The rich and powerful, in order to save their own pathetic lives and way of life, decided it was okay to destroy their own kind as long as they could take a bunch of us with them." He looked down at the children's book he paced across. "This proves that *all* humans have the capability within them to turn on each other. To rid themselves of the weak instead of protecting them as they should. There is no loyalty in humankind.

Chit stopped pacing, straightened up to his full height, and repeated what he'd said at the beginning of the conflict. "They *all* must die."

———

With the help of the newly arrived spaceships, dispatching the billions of remaining humans was easy. They no longer had a place to hide. They did have a better way to fight back, and the Entosadurians sustained some heavy casualties. But, in the end, it made no difference for the humans, the sheer numbers of Entosadurians made their attempts to fight back futile.

The few remaining humans, those with the greatest survival skills who just hid themselves away from the world, became sport for the Entosadurians. Hunting them down and killing them became a great competition in the new world.

Chit observed as a new batch of younglings fed on a rotting pile of human bodies. He shuddered as he thought about Hailey being used as fodder for the developing young of his own kind.

A cold chill ran down his exoskeleton, and he whispered, "Perhaps we are no better than the humans we annihilated. Perhaps we all deserve death…"

HOLLI ANDERSON

Holli Anderson has a Bachelor's Degree in Nursing—which has nothing to do with writing, except maybe by adding some descriptive injury and vomit scenes to her books. She discovered her joy of writing during a very trying period in her life when escaping into make-believe saved her. She enjoys reading any book she gets her hands on,  but has a particular love for anything fantasy. Holli is a member of the elite group, Space Balrogs, a troupe of authors who present hilarious interactive convention events.

Saved by H. L. Anderson

Theresa Kent is a wife, mom, and hard-working nurse living in rural Colorado. Life is good until her increasingly despondent, unemployed husband suddenly snaps--his vicious attack leaves Theresa fighting for her life as she tries to escape the insane version of the man she loves.

Ryan Tucker appears to have it all, except he's been merely existing, not living, for the the last three years. His emotions get a much needed jump start when he rescues Theresa from the torment her life has become in just a matter of days. Ryan feels an instant and fierce desire to protect this stranger that fell into his life.

Hanging over their heads is the knowledge that Theresa's husband is still out there, hunting for her.

Can two broken souls be repaired, or will the demons of the past and present come between the repressed love that grows between them?

Check out Holli's website:
www.holli-anderson.com

Find all of Holli's great books on Amazon:
amzn.to/2nYTps2

Like Holli on Facebook:
www.facebook.com/Author-Holli-Anderson-Author-HL-Anderson-338395009614151

Follow **@HaAuthor** on Twitter:
twitter.com/HaAuthor

IN A SECRET ROOM

D. J. Butler

"How long will you be gone, Doctor?"

"Don't call me by my given name. It isn't seemly."

Benson looks puzzled. "Your first name is David."

He doesn't say *Christian* name, and neither do I. That's deliberate.

I step into the center of the diagram, painted on the floor with the blood of still-living, flawless goats. The things the Hebrews never wrote down, but passed in secret whispers from father to daughter to son, would shock this world of electric lights and airplanes.

The diagram is painted on the wooden floor of a secret room inside the White House. Built originally for Washington's kabbalist Josiah Seixas, I have rediscovered it by the usual means: saffron-scented incense inscribed with the sign of the intelligence of Mercury, a ring of fixed quicksilver, a dowsing rod. The walls are thick enough to stop the sounds of animal sacrifice, and the door is hidden behind a painting of Lee surrendering at Appomattox. The room is lit with candles. I have layered multiple wards of misdirection to ensure that no one knows of the room's existence other than Benson and me.

"My parents named me *Doctor*, because I am a seventh son. It is one of the sources of my gift, as your gift comes from the vestigial tail amputated at birth from your own coccyx and worn dried around your neck. I call myself *David* in part to appear more mundane. As my apprentice, you must call me *Mister West*."

"I won't always be your padawan." Benson snivels.

I need a better apprentice, and in less pinched times, I'd have one. But first the WPA and now the war effort have sucked up much of the best magical talent, and as Roosevelt's personal occultist, the unofficial member of his cabinet hidden behind the words *and others*, I am in no position to complain about the President's call for resources.

"What in Hades is a *padawan?*"

Benson looks as if he's swallowed a bird. "It means an apprentice."

"You need to stop reading Crowley and the Theosophists," I tell him. "The nonsense they invent to fill the enormous gaps in their knowledge can only obscure the few grains of truth they actually possess. Try one of the Arabs. Abd al-Hazred or, better, al-Jildaki."

"Yes, Mr. West."

"I'll be gone only an hour, as you experience the passage of time. I'll enter the body of the vagrant I've identified using the Eye, then retrieve my staff and other accouterments from the wall of the boarding house."

This is serious magic, though Benson cannot grasp it. I will travel forward in time and enter the body of another man.

But the challenge is serious. Starting as early as I have, fortunately, if I fail, I have time to try again.

"And with your staff and seals," Benson says slowly, "you will be able to close the gate as soon as it is opened."

He is an idiot, but he's my apprentice. "Yes. That is the best moment, because the Old One's cult will have exhausted all its energy, spilt its precious blood, and taken its one shot. And then I will steal their victory from them."

"And save the world." Benson smiles.

"Yes."

"On December 21, 2020."

"The winter solstice. When the energies of this world are at their ebb, yes. As they are today, on this winter solstice, 1943."

"But what if they kill you?"

I shrug out of the silk robe resembling a long smoking jacket but embroidered ornately with the characters of a forgotten Chinese script, the words telling in poetic stanzas the story of my own life, and hand it to Benson. I am careful not to disturb any of the markings on the floor. This leaves me naked, as the magic requires. To ease my passage through the astral sphere and into a future configuration of the planets, I have also shaved all the hair from my body.

"If they kill me," I explain, virtually certain that I have explained this many times before, "then they only kill a vagrant drunk, and I return here to my time and body with seventy-seven years to marshal my resources and try again. As many as seventy-five more times, if need be."

"What does this have to do with the war?" Benson asks.

"Benson," I say. "Shut up."

Benson retreats to the corner of the five-sided room.

I lie in the center of the diagram. The wood floor of this room is ordinarily cold, since the furnace vents all stay far from it, but the wood now is hot to the touch; if my buttocks had any hair left, the floor would scorch it off. I endure without a murmur. This is the energy of the markings themselves. I can do no magic without a talisman, and here, to send myself a traveler to such a remote day, I have built a talisman the size of the room.

I close my eyes and chant the words. I invoke Jupiter, all the constellations and the great precession, and the *primum mobile* above all.

Abruptly, I am clothed.

I smell smoke and the reeks of urine and cheap alcohol, and a bitter wind digs at my skin through a cloak of rags. I drag myself to my feet, climbing up the brick wall beside me.

"Where you think you're going, Peterson?" growls a heap of rags at my feet.

I have no time for this. I turn and walk toward the boarding house.

I know immediately that this is solstice, in the year 2020. I know it because a cold, sticky mist that smells of bog and charnel fills the Mall. I keep the long grass to my left, circling around it toward where I have hidden my tools, seventy-seven years ago.

My borrowed flesh is stiff, from alcohol and years of abuse, from cold and from sleeping on sidewalks. Ah, well. The Eye shows me what it chooses, and not what I choose. I have selected this body because the Eye told me it would be here. I selected the boarding house for the same reason.

I stagger across concrete steps, and over ragged grass. Winter has left all the trees skeletal and angry.

From deep within the mist comes a rumbling sound, like thunder, only it is a thunder that carries words. I know enough of this language to know I must immediately clap my hands over my ears. I do so, but it is with an effort.

The mist glows red. Where the Washington Monument should be stands instead a ragged circle of inwardly-curving stone pillars. Like teeth.

The red glow illuminates the faces of the office buildings

and museums that enclose the Mall. As the Eye had shown me they would be, the buildings are all draped in bright red cloth. For the rite, to welcome the world-ending abomination the cult now tries to bring to Washington, D.C., the buildings have been converted to flags.

Nazi flags. The black swastikas on white circles glare like malevolent, welcoming eyes at the mist, and then the light dies.

The shrill, wet screams of sacrificial victims rise again as the Nazi Anierophants and Oneiromancers pour more human energy into the blasphemous cosmic womb from which they attempt to draw the beast.

I'll say this for them: if the Eye has shown me true visions, the cult at least had the wisdom—or the good taste—to kill all the congressmen and senators first.

"Who goes there?" a voice asks me curtly. "Papers?"

It's a Nazi officer. At least, he's wearing the crisp khakis and the armbands our boys are... were... fighting over in Europe. But his accent is depressingly American. He sounds like he could be from Indiana.

Fortunately, he thinks I'm drunk.

"Papersh." I stagger a bit, slur my words.

"Never mind." The Nazi from the Midwest smiles. "Come with me."

He reaches for me, obviously intending to go heap me on the pile of corpses exsanguinating a squirt of cosmic bread crumbs into the void. I head-butt him right in the nose, and when he drops to the grass, I pounce.

His screams might go unnoticed among the wailing of the doomed and the damned, but I won't take any chances. I grab him by the sides of his head and twist his neck sharply. The loud crack his neck makes as it breaks sickens me, but I have no choice.

The world is at stake.

The red glow returns and the rumble of thunder-speech. I clap my hands to my ears and stagger to the boarding house.

The building has barely survived to this date. It is now condemned, with red tape wrapped around the gap-toothed iron fence warning casual passersby away from the impending demolition.

I am not a casual passerby. I hop the fence—this is harder than I expect in my borrowed hobo's skin, and I fall on my face. Then I push through the front door, sagging off its hinges, and go directly to my room.

I hit the wall switch and a single bulb lights up, swinging from a length of wire overhead. I have seen this very room this morning... this morning, that is, in 1943. My wooden bed is gone, and my table. In their place are a cheap iron bedframe that is slowly rusting to nothing, and a slat-backed chair that is missing two slats and a leg.

Also, the wall has been torn open.

My vault, my repository. The place where I carefully sealed up staff, seals, ring, and cloak, to arm myself for the battle with the Nazi void demon, is revealed. I reach into the wall and feel around, hoping that I will find my tools, fallen into a shadowed corner.

My hope dies, instantly and brutally.

My things are gone. I am unarmed and defenseless.

"Perhaps you were looking for these," a voice behind me says.

I spin around, forgetting to even play the part of a homeless drunk. I don't know the face of the man confronting me; he might be a university professor, from his tweed jacket and scuffed black shoes. He raises a fire bucket to the height of his chest and overturns it. A cloud of black ashes sifts down, and falling rapidly from the cloud to the floor go shapeless lumps of silver and amber, torn scraps of cloth and leather, and scorched paper fragments.

My tools.

"No," I mutter. I slouch, trying to resume the appearance of a hobo. "I was lookin' fer a.... fer a bottle. Whishky?"

The man shakes his head. "Oh, Doctor West." He drops the bucket to the floor between us with a clank, and then I see the knife in his hand.

Not just any knife. The dull glint suggests meteoric iron, and the scratching hint at antediluvian names of old gods of death: Anubis, Odin, Nergal. I would like time to examine it more closely, but this knife is a tool of death. It may be a thing that can kill me permanently, despite my borrowed body.

I step into the bucket and launch it upward with my foot. The metal catches the professor in the jaw and hurls ash into his face. He staggers away, and I throw myself out the window.

As I am squeezing through, he catches my rag cloak. For a moment, I'm pinned, but then the rotting fabric tears and I'm through, onto the roof over the boarding house's front porch. He lunges after me and I dance away, to the edge of the rooftop, and the knife narrowly misses.

I scoot around the window frame and scramble up onto the roof above my room. My pursuer curses and climbs out after me. This is exhilarating, I can't lose, so long as he doesn't kill me with the dark death-god dagger. All I have to do is break my own neck—the beggar's neck—and I wake up again in my own body, inside the Roosevelt White House, seventy-seven years earlier.

But at the highest chimney of the house, I pause.

The screaming has reached a new feverish peak, and the dull red glow has become a blazing beacon, a reddish sun burning on the Mall as the old year dies.

I see the columns. There are thirteen of them, an unnatural number.

And I see the beast moving forward through the columns.

Where the beast comes from I cannot say—there is no visible gate behind it, and it appears to grow larger, or more solid, or more now, as if my eyes are witnessing a dimension of the cosmos they have never before seen, and my pitiful brain struggles to interpret the data it receives. Similarly, I cannot tell how many limbs the beast has or whether it has wings or tentacles. I see obscene fleshy membranes, and eyes on every surface, and mouths opening on hands and feet and belly. I see nothing resembling a head or a face. The beast looks in all directions. It looks at me, and into my heart.

Have I underestimated the challenge?

Should I have brought reinforcements?

The scratching of the professor's shoes on the shingles behind me warns me just in time. I tear my thoughts away from the incomprehensible blasphemy against the order of the universe that now crawls forth onto the Mall, tossing humans into its many maws....

And I duck.

The knife cuts through the air over my head. It misses, and still I feel a burning on my flesh where it almost makes contact. Years of study of the sweet science kick in, and I punch my attacker in his throat.

He falls to his knees, choking. He swings again, and misses.

He's off-balance, clinging to the shingles.

I punch him in the eye, and he goes rolling backward down the roof. His head strikes the chimney beneath him with a soggy thump, and he lies still.

I turn to regard the beast again. Is it walking? Crawling? Dragging itself forward on its elbows? I cannot tell. Perhaps the world shifts, hurling itself and its pathetic, candleflame-lived occupants into the many devouring maws of the beast.

It heaves itself upon the white house, which crumbles to the ground and erupts in sheets of flame.

Still it looks at me.

Shivering, I crouch. Still feeling the eyes on me, I descend the rooftop, hiding from the vision of those many eyes. This is the thing I have come here to defeat, and instead I have lost.

But this is only one round, and I have deliberately chosen a bout that will last many rounds. I have but to kill myself, return to my natural time and body, and try again.

I stop to examine the knife. I do not touch it but crouch over it on the boarding house rooftop. The glyphs are Lemurian and Atlantean, a horrible unlearned mishmash but magically-effective nonetheless. If only I could hide this inside a wall and find it in my own time when I return.... but clearly, I cannot.

Sighing, I stand. The shrieks are unbearable now. Thousands must be dying of slow torture this very moment. Or is the beast itself shrieking? Does its natural song sound like the dying howl of sacrificial offerings?

I will not look at it again. I do not need to.

Instead, I step to the edge of the rooftop and confirm the location of the wrought iron fence. Then I take a running leap and throw myself face-first toward the rusting spikes.

I feel the cold iron enter my borrowed neck and chest.

I awake, in my own flesh. The floor beneath my back and calves has grown cold. The candles sputter, their wicks nearly consumed.

"Benson," I croak.

There is a pause. "Yes?" Benson answers.

I ache. My throat and chest hurt from the wounds my host body has just now died of, seventy-seven years in the future. I sit up, shivering. "My robe. I feel cold."

"You're going to feel colder," Benson says. He stands in

the darkest corner of the room, his face in shadow and invisible.

"Impertinent pup!" I shout. "Now, of all times, you would play the idiot? I am done with you!"

I stand, stiffer and more awkward than ever I was in the hobo's flesh, and step toward the hook from which my robe hangs.

Improbably, I strike an invisible barrier.

I look down at the floor, and I see the diagrams I made. New markings enclose the old, and the new markings are wards of imprisonment and enclosure. Roaring wordlessly, I pound the unseen barrier. Stalking the star-shaped perimeter of the diagram, I test it with my fists and feet, shouting every counterspell and sacred name I know to shatter the spell that suddenly binds me.

"I *am* done," Benson agrees. "You see, I *have* read the Arabs. All of them. Many years ago."

I glare at him. "What do you want?"

"You have seen what I want." He steps forward, and in a final flicker of light, I see the light of alien moons within Benson's eyes. Then the candles die and darkness falls. "Everything I want is coming, Doctor. In seventy-seven years."

Doctor.

I have been betrayed.

I roar, but he says nothing more. I hear the secret passage that is the room's only entrance open and shut, without a glimmer of light.

We have all been betrayed.

The world ends in seventy-seven years. I have seen it.

But my world ends now. In darkness, alone.

I sit.

I will meditate to slow my breathing and my heart rate, ease my metabolic processes to a thread, whisper as I have learned to do from the yogins of Calcutta and Mayapore, but it will only delay the inevitable. Only Benson can find me, and Benson is my captor. My body will consume its fat, then its muscle, then its organs.

I will not be found.

My mummified corpse will be crushed to powder by the beast, on December 21, 2020. I have seen it, with borrowed eyes.

I lie on the floor and close my now-pointless eyes of flesh.

Could I have stopped this? Could I have seen the betrayal coming?

What in Hades is a *padawan*?

D. J. BUTLER

Dave used to be a lawyer, but he's mostly recovered. Now he teaches business acumen for a living, but he tries to focus as much of his time as he can on teaching his kids the art of awesomeness. Dave writes fantasy, science fiction, horror, and related genres for all audiences, and he performs theater, rock and roll, and comedy as one of the founding Space Balrogs. He has a forthcoming steampunk fantasy series for middle readers with Knopf. His books for adults include, among others, the ongoing action-horror serial Rock Band Fights Evil, and the 2012 Whitney Award finalist steampunk novel City of the Saints.

Witchy Eye by D. J. Butler

Sarah Calhoun is the fifteen-year-old daughter of the Elector Andrew Calhoun, one of Appalachee's military heroes and one of the electors who gets to decide who will next ascend as the Emperor of the New World. None of that matters to Sarah. She has a natural talent for hexing and one bad eye, and all she wants is to be left alone—especially by outsiders.

But Sarah's world gets turned on its head at the Nashville Tobacco Fair when a Yankee wizard-priest tries to kidnap her. Sarah fights back with the aid of a mysterious monk named Thalanes, who is one of the not-quite-human Firstborn, the Moundbuilders of the Ohio. It is Thalanes who reveals to Sarah a secret heritage she never dreamed could be hers.

Now on a desperate quest with Thalanes to claim this heritage, she is hunted by the Emperor's bodyguard of elite dragoons, as well as by darker things—shapeshifting Mockers and undead Lazars, and behind them a power more sinister still. If Sarah cannot claim her heritage, it may mean the end to her, her family—and to the world where she is just beginning to find her place.

Check out Dave's website:
davidjohnbutler.com

Find all of Dave's Mind-Bending Books on Amazon:
amzn.to/2MIYhzz

Like Dave on Facebook:
www.facebook.com/dave.butler.16

Follow **@DavidJohnButler** on Twitter:
twitter.com/DavidJohnButler

THE EIGHTH DAY

Robert J Defendi

So . . . here I am.

There is only one way in or out of this room. It's a door, one-and-a-half meters thick, made from solid, alloyed titanium. There are people on the other side of this door, and they want me dead.

But that door is made out of one of the strongest materials known to man. It weighs at least thirty tons, and it's imbedded in thirty kilo-liters of inert hydraulics. These hydraulics add even more pressure to the weight of the door. The titanium can resist anything short of heat in the order of twenty-five thousand degrees Celsius, such as ground zero at a thermonuclear explosion.

I estimate it will buy me about three hours.

I'm getting ahead of myself. I sit before the mainframe of the most sophisticated computer ever built. All I can think to do is write. I enjoy writing. I'd like to think that I'm good at it, but let's let posterity decide.

Here it goes. Once upon a time, (I've always wanted to start a story like that. I know it's considered trite, but these are my last few hours so I won't ever know what people think of it.) Where was I . . . oh, yes. Once upon a time, (These parenthetical intrusions may become irritating. Ignore them if they distract you. I know they distract me.)

Once upon a time, (time and time again) I found myself in Phoenix. Now Phoenix is one hell of a place, but summer had come so it was hotter than that plasma torch that's making the titanium door drip away like the seconds of my life. (All right, maybe that was pretty bad, what are you going to do about it, huh?) I sat in a bar. (I don't drink, but you can find good work in bars. Not to mention entertainment. You know, the hot, sweaty, I-Promise-I'll-Respect-You-In-The-Morning type of entertainment that I'll stop describing. Children will read this. Hell, everyone will read this.) A man approached me with a proposition. (The type that's illegal, not immoral. It wasn't that kind of a bar.) He said that society was sick. Well, I could see his point. I mean, society is more than a little queasy, and it could use a good physician, but Doctor Martin Luther King Jr. has been dead damn near a century, and modern doctors drug your problems away. Society seems to be doing a pretty good job of that on its own. (I don't touch artificial substances. As a mercenary, I could always take down some bozo riding a sub easier than one not. Even those combat jobs.)

So . . . he had this plan to destroy society. 'What about afterwards?' I ask. 'Anything would be better!' he said. Well, I didn't know about that, but I asked him what he intended to do, 'I mean, society is a pretty big critter. Are you gonna kill it outright or just hamstring it?' Well, after I explained my colloquialisms, (That's a word he understood, 'Book learned!' my great grand-daddy would've said) he told me what he wanted me to do. I laughed at him. Then he quoted my pay.

I stopped laughing.

Now, until that moment, I hadn't taken the anarchist seriously. But if he could offer me that much, then he had enough money to finance his plan. Now, I'm not sure if this job amounted to the noble deed he thought, but that was a lot of gold. I mean a lot of gold. I think it weighed more than my flat. I know it weighed more than my car.

So I said yes.

He gave me a tenth in advance. I outfitted myself through my supplier, then considered a trip to Acapulco. Hell, I could buy Acapulco. All right, I may be exaggerating, but hell, it's my story, and it was a hell of a lot of gold.

I went pretty mainstream (albeit state of the art) when it came to weapons. Two .8mm, fully automatic, Beretta Flechette Launchers, one for each hand. This was the Gauss model, and electro-magnetic propulsion has a tremendously fast firing rate, so I also bought sixteen hundred each, of standard, poison, knockout, armor piercing, and explosive flechettes. I decided against an assault rifle. I mean, the Beretta .8mm has comparable stopping power, and I couldn't carry any more ammo anyway. I had the pistols altered to fit my cybernetic idiosyncrasies.

Then I decided to have a little fun. Now, Ex-Corp recently came out with a new suit of combat armor. It's a light, flexible, crystal-polymer matrix, nearly indestructible, with a sensory network that you can jack straight in or wire through your cybernetics. The suit itself encumbered less than kevlar and could withstand hundreds of thousands of foot-pounds before tearing. Anodized polymer made up the helmet, and it could resist impacts that would probably break your neck. It bestowed three hundred and sixty degree vision (Something that you have to experience to believe). It had normal, infra-red, low-lite, and telescopic capabilities, and to top it all off, I had a H.U.D. to play with. (H.U.D. is an antiquated acronym standing for Heads Up Display. I used to fly antique jets. Really the helmet just plugged into the neuro-jacks in the back of my cranium.)

To round out my arsenal, I bought ten canisters of neuro-toxin. As an afterthought, I bought a load of High Explosive Armor Piercing grenades. I had to go to Miami, and I wanted to prepare for traffic.

I thought about buying a backpack tactical nuke. I mean, I could afford it, but fissionable materials weigh a lot, and I value mobility. Besides, with my suit's environmentals I could survive nearly anything. I really didn't want to take in something that could kill me when they probably couldn't. In hindsight, I wish I had. (Deterrence my ass, I'm just a poor loser.)

I had to pick up an envelope. I climbed into my car, engaged the turbines and took off. At five-thousand feet I leveled off and opened her up. I flew above low-level traffic but below commercial air. It's an experience, you know. Jacked into the autopilot, I *became* the car. The turbines my legs. The control surfaces my arms. It's the closest thing there is to true freedom.

Freedom. What is freedom, anyway? A new bit of tech? A moment off the net? We've become a goddamn technocracy. We live on the datastream. We eat silicon and breathe binary. We rely on machines to the point where they've become more integral than our own arms. But then again, my arms *are* machines. I wonder if that's symbolic.

But I wax poetic.

Whatever the hell that means.

I landed in Miami two hours later. I picked up my packages and took off again. My next leg would take me to Nevada, and I would arrive there almost four hours after I'd left Phoenix. I climbed back into my beautiful car and flew the rest of the trip.

I landed in the desert and hoofed it. It was a good five klicks, and the walk helped me work the knots out of my back and legs. They didn't make the place easy to find, but the envelope came complete with digital maps and 3D schematics. I heard once that only a handful of people know the facility's actual location. I hoped that would cut down my opposition. (I'm just glad the damn place wasn't in Geneva, like I'd heard.)

The perimeter fence was a dark zapper (you know, the kind that really screw up the neurons. Some kind of headache, huh, boss?), so I had to wire a brown loop. (I'm very good at that sort of thing.) As the brown loop faded the field, I stepped through confidently. I switched to infrared and inched through the network of detection beams. About halfway across the yard I picked up a guard on the opposite building, a virgin by the signature. I clicked to low-lite and locked a targeter through my H.U.D. I shifted to standard flechettes and squeezed off one hundred and thirty-six rounds in a short burst. His head toppled cleanly off his shoulders. (I love this suit. It was worth the five million six that I paid for it.)

Electro-magnetic propulsion is quiet, so I went unnoticed.

I estimated that I had five minutes.

I was wrong . . . I had seven.

The front door made for a more difficult bypass, but after two minutes, I was in. (I'd like to tell you exactly how I do this, but I don't think that it would do you much good at this point.) Once inside, I shut the door and bypassed the recognition circuits, locking it until fixed. I doubt it will be anytime soon. (You see I placed a piece of cellophane tape between two leads. That's a nearly invisible, not to mention sadistic, way to screw up electronics.)

The main hall had its security, and I really didn't see any way to bypass it, so I just walked straight in. My H.U.D. read six minutes. Sloppy, I should have been there in four, but obviously they hadn't found the body yet and didn't realize I assaulted the place until the hall security picked me up. At least I wasn't the only sloppy one.

I believe my H.U.D. read seven minutes and six seconds when I met the first wave of resistance. I came around the corner, and they stood farther down the hall about twenty meters ahead of me. I didn't roll or anything. That was my first mistake: relying too heavily on my toys. I had cut the first two in half, mortally wounded the third, and was royally screwing up the vitals on the fourth when the fifth opened up. I didn't think he could respond that fast. He probably rode a sub, most likely a combat job.

Now this armor is good. I could feel his body heat through the sensory net. I could read his vital signs through a translator circuit in my infrared. I could register the temperature of his muzzle flashes. I could estimate the velocity and force of the bullets as they impacted with my armor. However, as the matrix absorbed the inertia of the fifty caliber rounds, spreading bruises and cracking ribs, I couldn't keep my feet.

To top it all off, I landed wrong. My spine absorbed the full shock, and my breath whooshed out of my lungs, adding insult to my injuries. I started thrashing about and watched my vitals go way out of control.

I was like that when he killed me.

Just kidding! Actually, I raised my Beretta, clicked in an explosive flechette, and squeezed it off into his mouth, hitting him in the soft pallet and turning his head into a fine red mist with pink-grey chunks that reminded me absurdly of tofu. Funny thing, that.

I arched my back, releasing the pressure on my diaphragm and allowing air to fill my lungs. This isn't as easy as it sounds, especially with broken ribs. I became dizzy and must have blacked out, but when I came to less than a minute had passed. The pain editor in my suit's bio-chip worked at full overclock, and already the edge came off the agony. In moments I rose, back on my feet.

(Perhaps I should explain something about my cybernetics. You may be wondering how I performed that ammo change. Two years ago, I had both my arms ripped off by a jealous lover. Luckily, my credit chip sat fluid from a recent job. I received medical care, and they even brought me around long enough to customize my cyberware. I couldn't afford any decent weapons, but there's still plenty of cyber in this punk. My arms are capable of storing up to five different types of ammunition and still manage selective feeds. Let me give you an example. My flechettes, packed, are less than one millimeter thick. In one arm I can pack five lines of eight hundred rounds each. They're fed through my palm directly into each gun. This is the only reason I could use these Berettas. In a clip, you couldn't contain enough ammunition to sustain five seconds of fire. It's a handy thing to have as a merc.)

Okay. Now, maybe I shouldn't have pumped that explosive flechette into him. I mean, the standard rounds only generate a high frequency buzz, but they had to know I'd arrived by then, and besides, he pissed me off.

Anyway . . . that's when they tried to gas me. Ten tons of metal crashed down on either side of me and the corridor filled with toxins, probably contact, almost definitely fatal. Of course, my armor protected me. I pulled out my portable tool kit, cut through the panel, and ran a bypass.

I was on my way again.

I had been on my assault for twenty minutes when I hit wave three of the defenses. They barricaded the corridor and laid suppressing fire on the hall. I threw a nerve gas canister and stepped over their twitching bodies, careful not to slip in the blood that squirted from their pores.

At the next barricade they wore gas masks. My neurotoxin requires only exposed skin. This time I slipped.

Moments later, I picked up the slight vibration of footsteps. Someone stalked me. I continued until I stood in the middle of a long, deserted hall. Then I waited.

He came around the corner and stood to face me. He wore body armor similar to my own. I clicked to armor piercing flechettes and hit him with a sustained burst. It forced him back several steps. His burst almost set me on my ass and ground the ends of my ribs together. Luckily my suit's bio-chip compensated by blocking my pain centers. I hate relying on that, but sometimes it's necessary.

We both knew the score. Our armor was impenetrable but completely flexible. A bullet couldn't penetrate it, and the kinetic energy of even the most powerful of handguns is less than that of a punch to the nose. A bullet's power resides in how concentrated its energy is applied, which makes it easy to drill through flesh. Take that energy and fire it into a substance that it can't penetrate, and the force becomes distributed. The bottom line is that a good swift kick would do more damage, because this armor boiled down to nothing more than a really tough suit of clothes.

I dropped my guns and approached him. He had a rank and insignia on his armor. He probably ran security. Or maybe he was their hired ringer. I don't know, but I doubt that they had many of these suits.

I started with a punch. You know, to kind of test the waters. He blocked easily and returned with a kick. I blocked it but didn't try anything fancy.

Then it started. He hit me with a flurry of attacks, beating down my guard and forcing me back. I had a difficult time returning the assault as he pressed down on me.

He was good.

I slipped through his guard, hitting him hard in the

helmet, jerking his head back but not enough to break his neck . . . unfortunately. He stumbled back a step. I stomped my foot, pulling his attention down, then punched for his face plate again, kicking him in the nuts as he blocked.

It didn't faze him. That's when I realized that he rode a substance. A combat job. A good one.

He came back, all over me. He had me on the defensive again. It was bad, and I breathed real heavy-like. I didn't know if I would survive.

I did, of course.

I spun, putting all the power I had behind a cybernetic backhand. It caught him across the face, knocking him sideways a step. Now, I know, you're probably wondering why I did this. You might think that it had no effect. Well, you're wrong. Every time I hit him in the face, it pissed him off. Normally there wouldn't be much benefit in that. The man was a pro. However, he rode a sub, and I could tell he rode it to the edge. So I forced myself through his guard again, jabbing him in the face.

He snapped.

As he came at me I stepped aside, kicking him full in the gut, splintering his ribs like brittle twigs and sending the shards through his lungs. As he doubled over, coughing, I only had a second.

I kicked him full in the head, picking up his body and flipping it over on his back. He died instantly, his neck snapped.

So . . . I was on my way again.

Forty minutes into my assault found me running a bypass on that very door that protects me now.

My sensory net picked up the vibration, even with all the abuse that it had taken, long before my ears heard the noise. (I bought a microwave from Ex-Corp once. I've had it five years and it has never needed a repair.) The door was in the blind wall of a T-intersection and troops snuck down all three halls. (Remember my helmet?) I spun and started mowing down the first wave with my Berettas, killing them pretty easily. Both guns clicked dry, and I shifted to knock-out darts.

I could feel the vibration without aid now.

But these troops were pretty persistent critters. They had to have been on combat subs. By that time I had worked completely through poison ammo and clicked to armor piercing.

It was then I saw the tank.

Five seconds later I saw the cyborg.

I didn't know which was worse. With my left hand I started pumping A.P. darts through the tank, while my right hand riddled the cyborg. I couldn't see much effect, and I think the only human thing left in that cyborg was the brain.

I raised my Beretta for a head shot.

At that moment the tank fired as it swerved into the wall, its crew dead. The round hit me full in the head, distracting me as the cyborg grabbed me under the arms, crushing my rib cage.

I probably would have been dead then, but the tank crew had underestimated a normal tank round's ability to kill me. I don't care if my armor would have withstood it, but if I had been hit by the force of a standard depleted uranium tank shell, you would have been hard pressed to find two bones in me more than a half an inch long.

As it was, they had fired one of those robot, gyro-rounds. You know, the kind that *drill* through armor. I could see the round drilling toward my right eye and blanked out a moment as the cyborg splintered my remaining rib-cage. My arms thrashed about as my pain editor tried to compensate, twitching as my Berettas dumped their rounds into the walls.

Two more ribs cracked, (and I thought they had all broken. What a pleasant surprise!) causing me to spit blood across my visor, tinting my vision red. I watched the dust from the gyro-round sift down next to my right eye. My guns fired explosive rounds now, riddling the wall with little zit holes and making a sound like a high-speed drum roll.

I threw down my pistols and reached up, ripping my helmet off, destroying the seals and breaking my nose in the process. I barely had enough presence of mind to point the bottom of the helmet at the head of the cyborg. The round drilled through and crashed into the other side of the helmet, detonating.

The force of the explosion ripped the helmet from my grasp and hit the cyber-thing full in the face, caving in its skull and squirting its brain out of its audio receptors. I fell to the ground, trying to gasp, trying to breathe. The pain soared beyond my bio-chip's ability to compensate. Waves of nausea and euphoria rippled through my body as my suit pumped endorphins and pain killers into my system. That was all I needed. I don't like using them, (they screw up your reflexes) but they slowly brought the pain under control and I hovered on the edge of passing out. Other chemicals are holding off the effects of shock. That's kept me going, but the pain is still there, still overwhelming, and even the breath it takes to dictate this story is a constant reminder.

It was over.

Almost.

I finished my bypass and picked up my helmet. It would protect my head, and I still could see out of it normally, but otherwise it was a total write-off. I pulled the disk they had given me in the envelope out of the storage panel in my helmet. It appeared undamaged. I slid it into the mainframe and accessed it. I checked my time. I had left Phoenix six hours and fifty-eight minutes before.

Now, they say that, including his rest, God created the Earth in seven days. I had just destroyed it in under seven hours.

And now that I sit here, I wonder why I did it. I mean, I really wonder. There's the job. The mission and all that. But those are just, I don't know. Words. Excuses. Sounds. At the end of the day, they don't mean anything. They are hollow.

The gold will still be there, and it will probably become the new monetary system, but I'll never see it. My car will still be there, and it won't be affected, but I'll never drive it. I don't even know who the anarchist was, and I never will.

As I sit here, probably dying, I can't help but get religious. My parents raised me Lutheran. They say that God created the world in six days, then rested. They say the solar system is over six billion years old. Some say that God's days are a billion years long.

When God wakes up, he's going to be pissed.

I wonder if that has anything to do with it.

Now that's the stupidest thing I've ever heard.

Anyway, there's probably an army on the other side of that door. They're within minutes of cutting through. My helmet's screwed, cooked, and air conditioned, but it will still protect my head. I have eight canisters of neuro-toxin left, but I can't use them without killing myself now that I've lost environmental integrity. I have twenty grenades, but that won't be enough. I have one-hundred-and-thirty-eight explosive flechettes left. I fired the rest into the walls.

I can promise you one thing. They don't intend to take me alive.

I don't stand a chance in hell.

That's what it's all about, though, isn't it? Some people fear hell. Some people love hell. Some people raise hell. Some people go to hell. Some people are mad as hell. What the hell does it all mean?

Somebody, when talking about America, once told us to beware, for there is no afterlife for a place that began as heaven.

You know, it just occurred to me that some of you may not have figured it out yet.

It's all about communication. That's the backbone of any society. You can't have civilization without it. Nowadays civilization has brought communication to the level of an art form. Everything connects with everything else, even the electronic door latches. Nothing is isolated, and it's all routed through one system. Now, this system is backed up better than any network ever. Any segment of this net can take over at any given time. Nobody can destroy this system.

But this system can destroy society.

There is an old type of computer program called a 'virus.' All computers are protected against it these days, but the disk that I just accessed three hours ago has the most sophisticated virus ever created. It could only work here, at the active mainframe, but now the most powerful electronic brain ever created will use every resource available to keep you out of the system. You'll never crack it.

So . . . every time you try to use the phone, every time you try to use your computers, every time you try to program your food dispensers, every time you try to start your cars, every time you try to open your doors . . .

All you will get is this story.

They're about to break through the door now. The hole they're cutting is nearly complete.

Good bye.

Good luck.

ROBERT J DEFENDI

Robert J Defendi was one of the writers for Savage Seas for the game Exalted. He's worked on Spycraft, Shadowforce Archer and the Stargate SG-1 roleplaying game. He wrote the current incarnation of Spacemaster. As the publisher of Final Redoubt Press, he designed and released the critically  acclaimed setting The Echoes of Heaven. He was featured in Writers of the Future XIX, and When Darkness Comes. He's the author of the successful podcast audiobook Death by Cliché. He's featured in Space Eldritch, Space Eldritch II, and Redneck Eldritch, as well as Actuator 3: Chaos Chronicles and the Curiosity Quills: Darkscapes anthology.

Robert J Defendi was born in Dubuque, IA (in accordance with prophecy). He reads voraciously, if you consider audiobooks reading (which you shouldn't). He has yet to find, conquer, and rule a small Central American country (but I think we all know that's inevitable). He is neither Team Jacob nor Team Edward (he is sympathetic to Team Guy-Who-Almost-Hit-Bella-With-A-Truck). He shamelessly stole that last joke.

Death by Cliché by Bob Defendi

To Sartre, Hell was other people. To the game designer, Hell is the game.

Damico writes games for a living. When called in to rescue a local roleplaying game demo, Damico is shot in the head by a loony fan. He

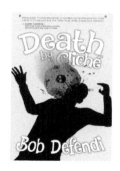

awakens in a game. A game full of hackneyed tropes and clichéd plots. A game he was there to save, run by the man who murdered him just moments ago. A game that has just become world-swap fantasy. Damico, to his horror, has become the heart of the cliché.

Set on their quest in a scene that would make Ed Wood blush, Damico discovers a new wrinkle. As a game designer, he is a creative force in this broken place. His presence touches the two-dimensional inhabitants. First a peasant, then a barmaid, then his character's own father...all come alive.

But the central question remains. Can Damico escape, or is he trapped in this nightmare? Forever.

Wait, what? This is a comedy? Ignore all that. Death by Cliché is a heartwarming tale of catastrophic brain damage. Share it with someone you love. Or like. Or anyone at all. Buy the book.

Based on a true story.

Check out Bob's Website:
www.robertjdefendi.com

Find all of Bob's Game-a-licious stories on Amazon:
amzn.to/2Lklovx

Like Bob on Facebook:
www.facebook.com/robertjdefendi

Follow **@RobertJDefendi** on Twitter:
twitter.com/robertjdefendi

OBJECT OF AFFECTION

Jason King

Jackson Keller sat at the small table opposite the redheaded woman with glasses. She carried a few extra pounds, but her green eyes and dimples more than compensated for the double chin and drumstick legs. Of course, Jackson couldn't say anything. He was a hundred pounds overweight, with curly hair currently in the style of a "white-guy-fro" and had a conspicuous mustard stain on his snug-fitting Captain America tee.

"So, what's your name?" Jackson asked.

The redhead's smile faltered, and she motioned at her nametag. "Vicki."

"Right." Jackson tensed. He was not off to a good start. "I'm Jackson."

"I know," Vicki said.

Jackson looked down at his nametag. "Right. So, um, tell me about you."

Vicki forced a nervous laugh. "Well, I'm a customer support concierge for Labtech."

Jackson snorted. "Concierge? You mean you work in a call center."

Vicki frowned. "Sure. I guess. Anyway, I love cats. My favorite singer is Taylor Swift, and I love ice cream."

"I can see that." Jackson chuckled.

Vicki hesitated for a long, uncomfortable moment before forcing out. "Tell me about you."

Jackson grinned. "Well, I'm a tier-two IT support agent for StarTel, and I'm a level 78 necro-caster on Fated Worlds. I live with my mom and little sister, and have the biggest collection of Dragon Ball Z figures in the county—I have a certificate to prove it. My online moniker is Firestorm4728, and I dominate at Star Wars trivial pursuit. Do you know how many Dewbacks were in the original 1977 theatrical cut of the first Star Wars movie?"

"Not... really..." Vicki glanced pleadingly to the girl at the neighboring table.

Jackson held up two fingers. "Dos!"

Vicki just stared at him. After another long moment she said, "I need to go to the bathroom." Then she stood and left. That was the third time that'd happened to Jackson that evening. He sighed, pulled out his phone, and checked for Pokemon. He'd seen a Scyther around there and was checking if it was still there.

"Excuse me, sir."

Jackson looked up to find the host glaring down at him. The guy had one of those stupid side shaved but long on top cuts complete with hipster glasses, neatly trimmed beard, and flannel shirt.

"What?" Jackson looked back at his phone.

"I think you should go."

Jackson's head snapped back up. "But I paid fifty bucks to be here!"

The hipster lumberjack nodded. "For which we will refund you."

Jackson stood. "Why?!"

His raised voice made the host glance around uncomfortably. "We've had complaints."

Jackson looked at the others in the room. Everyone had fallen silent and was staring at him. He pocketed his phone and nodded. "Ok. Yeah. Fine. I get it."

Jackson made for the door but stopped just before exiting and turned back to the others in the room. He grabbed his gut, jiggled it, and yelled, "Ya'll just can't handle this much sexy!"

The room of speed daters jeered at him, to which Jackson responded by giving them the double bird salute as he backed through the exit.

Jackson didn't have a car, and he didn't want to call his mom to pick him up early because he'd have to explain to her why he'd been kicked out of speed dating—again. So he put his hands in the pockets of his low hanging cargo shorts and began the long walk home.

Thirty-six and Jackson wasn't married. He hadn't ever had a girlfriend. Well, unless he counted Suzie Saunders from kindergarten. But she'd dumped him during second recess for Bobby Jensen. Two-timing bitch. No, anime pillow and wall hangings aside, he hadn't even kissed a girl. Perhaps it was time to face the haunting fact he'd ignored for years. He was a loser.

A tear slipped down Jackson's cheek. It didn't make sense. His mom always told him just how handsome he was and would go on about how lucky some girl would be to have him. Uncle Jimmy said those things too and even cat-called him and would goose him during family parties after having one too many beers. So, clearly, he wasn't without *some* charm! So, why did no woman want him?

These thoughts—and some horrifying repressed memories of Uncle Jimmy—swirled in Jackson's mind as he walked. An hour into his metropolitan hike, he realized he didn't know where he was. He spun about, panic rising along with the bile in his throat. Last time he'd been lost a homeless man had chased him for three blocks, and he'd had to hide in a dumpster to lose him.

He whipped out his phone, about to tell Google to call his mom, when something caught his attention so completely that it dispelled his anxiety. It was a small tattoo parlor, it's neon light chasing away the dark of the night with an angry, alternating red and purple sign that read, "Nat's Tats." Maybe what he needed was a tattoo. Chicks loved tattoos! He had nothing to base that on, but it sounded right.

Jackson put away his phone and strolled confidently into the parlor. It was a claustrophobic room with an abandoned counter and an empty, repurposed dentist's chair. Plastered all over the walls were patterns, mostly variations on naked women and skull themes.

"Hello?" Jackson called. "Nat?"

A woman emerged from a beaded curtain behind the counter. She was older, but voluptuous and clad in sexy black leather. Her hair was purple, and she wore an overabundance of black eye-liner. Her nose and bottom lip were pierced, and tattoos ran from around the back of her neck down into her cleavage.

Jackson stared, mouth agape.

The woman smiled. "Well hello there, handsome."

Jackson stammered, "I-I want a tattoo."

The woman slinked from behind the counter and stood in front of Jackson, her body intimately close to his—as though they were lovers.

"And why would a sweet boy like you want to defile his alabaster skin with the devil's ink?"

Jackson wrinkled his brow. "Don't you want my business?"

The woman flashed a black lipstick smile and raised a

hand to Jackson's face. She traced his cheek with long, black fingernails. He closed his eyes and shuddered.

"I want a tattoo so girls will like me," he breathed out.

The woman withdrew her hand and Jackson opened his eyes.

"I have something better." The leather clad woman took Jackson by the hand and led him behind the counter and through the beaded curtain.

His heart pounded, and his cheeks flushed. Maybe he was *about* to get a woman... or a disease. They entered a small room in the back of the parlor where, to his disappointment, there was no bed, just a stool next to a shelf full of strange objects.

A palm-sized silver skull with sapphire eyes, a jar enclosing a dead lizard floating in brown liquid, a candelabra made to look like a claw, a book entitled Demon Summoning in three easy steps, and a number of small occult-ish statues. If Jackson didn't know better, he'd say this woman was a—

"Witch," she said, as though finishing his thought. "Yes. I'm a witch."

Jackson's eyes widened. "Cool..."

The woman let go of his hand and sashayed over to her shelf filled with oddities. "So, you wish to attract a mate, do you Jackson?"

"Whoa! How do you know my name?"

The witch cocked a carefully penciled eyebrow. "Your name tag."

Jackson glanced down at his shirt where he still wore the sticker that read *Hi, my name is Jackson!*

He chuckled. "Oh yeah."

The witch examined her collection of small statues. "I can help you get a woman, or several. Whichever you desire."

"How?"

The witch selected one of her small statues, and winked at Jackson. "Magic."

"Well, I hope you're a high-level caster, because it's gonna take a lot of manna to make me someone a woman would want to be with."

The witch presented Jackson a three-inch obsidian statue of a nude woman. The tiny figurine had long flowing hair that fell to her feet and covered her naughty bits.

"What's this?" Jackson reached out a hand to take the statue, but the witch drew it back.

He rolled his eyes. "How much?"

The witch flashed a yellow-toothed grin. "Not much. Just some of your blood."

"My blood?!"

"Just a drop or two, in order to activate the magic and bind it to you." The witch reached behind her with her free hand and pulled a knife that must've been nestled in the small of her back, hidden by her waist-length purple hair.

Jackson's chest tightened, and he put up his hands to shield himself as he backed away. "I don't know what kind of kinky—"

The witch slashed the knife across his open palm.

Jackson sucked in a hiss through his teeth. "Son of a—"

Then the leather-clad witch put the small black statue into Jackson's bleeding hand and forced his fingers closed around it. "Alias passiones huius ignis non est sanguis!"

Jackson gasped at the red glow that flashed in the witch's eyes. It was quick enough that he was comfortably able to doubt whether he'd actually seen it.

"How is this supposed to get me chicks?"

The witch grinned but said nothing. She stared at Jackson. *Are her teeth sharper?*

"I'm gonna go now," he said. "Thanks for the statue."

Jackson backed through the beaded curtain, turned, and

ran out of the shop. After another block, he gave up trying to find his way home and called his mom to come pick him up.

———

Jackson woke the next day to find the black statue of the naked woman resting on his headboard staring at him. Had he put it there? He couldn't remember doing it. He glanced at the clock and swore. His shift started in ten minutes, and he'd overslept.

In lieu of a shower, Jackson suffused himself with body spray, changed his boxers and threw on his usual polo shirt and khaki combo. He was almost out of his room when he glanced back at the little woman statue watching him from her perch on his headboard. He looked at the cut on his hand, now surrounded by angry red skin.

"What the hell?" Jackson shrugged and snatched the statue and slipped it in his pocket.

A fight with his mother over the deplorable state of his basement bedroom delayed Jackson further and he was a full fifteen minutes late by the time his mom dropped him off in front of the office building that hosted StarTel.

He swiped his ID badge at the security desk, catching a headshake from the guard posted there.

"Late again, Keller. That's the third time this month. Findley's gonna have your balls in a jar on her desk!"

Jackson flipped-off the guard who chuckled good-naturedly.

Jackson very nearly made it to his desk unnoticed but froze when he heard his supervisor's voice call out to him.

"Keller! In my office, now!"

Jackson gritted his teeth and ignored the tongue clucking from the guy in the neighboring cubicle.

"Ms. Findley, I can explain," Jackson said as he closed the

office door behind him.

Sandi Findley was a no-nonsense, middle-aged blonde woman always dressed in a pants suit. She was a lead trainer with a reputation as a ball-buster, and Jackson gulped as he expected a demonstration.

Findley sat behind her desk staring at Jackson over her bifocals. "This is the third time you've been late this month, Keller."

"I know, I know. And I'm super sorry."

"Quiet!" Findley snapped. "It just so happens to be time for your semi-annual evaluation. Sit."

Crap. Jackson sat. He glanced around nervously. Why had she drawn down her office window's blinds?

"As you know, we score you on a list of attributes, one being the lowest and five the highest. Too many ones and you're fired." Findley tapped on her tablet and swiped to the left. She glanced at Keller then back to her tablet and started reading. "Technical Knowledge, three. Team collaboration, two. Punctuality, one."

Jackson bowed his head. *I'm gonna get fired for sure.*

"Customer satisfaction, two. Initiative, one. Workstation cleanliness, two, and appearance... five plus."

Jackson looked up to find Findley smirking at him.

"Five plus?" Jackson glanced down at his wrinkled polo and a ranch stain on his pants.

"Mmm hmm," Findley purred. She took off her glasses and reached behind her head, and a heartbeat later her hair fell down around her shoulders.

"Uhh...." was all Jackson could manage.

Findley stood, swept piles of paper off her desk with a hand and climbed onto it. She crawled across the desk and leaned in close to Jackson, her face only inches from his.

"You look absolutely delicious today, Jackson Findley," she said in a breathy voice.

"Well I did have a donut this..."

Findley rammed her lips onto his, and began to passionately kiss him.

An hour later Jackson left Findley's office, walking in a daze to his desk. That had been completely unexpected. And completely... AWESOME!

Jackson wiped lipstick from his chin and grinned.

Two more female co-workers threw themselves at Jackson before the day was over. It was surreal, like something from his pathetic midnight fantasies. What was going on? That's when Jackson remembered the statue in his pocket. He pulled it out and examined the tiny nude woman sculpted from obsidian. Could the witch's magic have actually been real? What other explanation was there?

His mom pulled up to the curb in front of his office, and Jackson caught three attractive girls staring at him as he got in the car. Upon making eye-contact with one, she winked. Holy crap, this was actually happening.

"How was your day Jacky?" his mom asked.

"Good." Jackson nodded. "Very good."

That night Jackson's phone blew up with text messages from female acquaintances. How they'd gotten his number, he had no clue. None of them had given him theirs and in several cases he'd asked. Along with the texts came a plethora of heart and lips emojiis, steamy talk, and naughty pictures. Whatever that witch had done to Jackson, he had now become an estrogen magnet.

Life was good.

The sound of shattering glass awakened him. Jackson sat up in his bed and looked around, only to find a woman in a trench coat climbing in through his broken window without any regard for the pieces of glass slicing her bare feet. She slipped on her own blood, but caught herself and finally, and not so gracefully, landed on his floor where she stood facing his bed.

"Hey!" Jackson shouted. Well, more screamed in a high-pitched voice than shouted. "Who the hell are you?!"

The woman made a mock pouting expression. "You don't remember me, Jacky?"

"Vicki from speed dating?"

Vicki smiled and took a slow seductive step forward. "I just couldn't stop thinking about you and had to see you."

"You could've just face-timed me."

"I know," Vicki said. "But it just isn't the same." She undid the belt of her trench coat and opened it to reveal she was wearing only a lacy black bra and panties.

For a larger woman, Jackson thought she pulled the look off pretty good. Then he saw the blood pooling at her feet. "Doesn't that hurt?"

"Not as much as being without you, Jacky." Vicki shrugged off the trench coat, climbed onto the bed, and slowly crawled toward him.

Jackson scooted back until his headboard stopped him. Something was very wrong with this girl. "Mom!" Jackson screamed.

Vicky put a finger to her lips. "Shhh! We don't want to be interrupted."

"Yes, we do! MOM!" Jackson screamed.

His bedroom door flew open, kicked in by a short woman wearing a bathrobe, giant pink curlers, and holding a shotgun.

"Mom, help!" Jackson's voice pitched embarrassingly high.

Jackson's mother pumped the shotgun and ordered, "Get off of my baby, you hussy!"

Vicky's eyes widened, and she slowly scooted off the bed.

An hour later, Jackson found himself sitting to the side of a police officer's desk, recounting his embarrassing story for the eighteenth time that night, whilst the woman officer typed up his words on her computer.

"And can you describe what your assailant was wearing?"

Jackson sighed. "Trench coat and then just a bra and panties."

"What color?"

Jackson furrowed his brow. "Black? I guess."

"Like this?" The officer unbuttoned her shirt to give Jackson a generous view of her chest and the black bra she wore.

"Oh hell." He tried to stand, but the officer deftly locked a cuff onto his wrist and the other cuff onto the arm of the chair.

"You're not going anywhere, loverboy." She glanced around the room furtively and then leaned in close. "I think there's an interview room no one's using. Let's go, and I'll show you some better ways to use those handcuffs."

"Help!" Jackson croaked. "Someone help!"

The desk sergeant—a large black woman—and a skinny male officer both turned to look at Jackson. "Help me!"

"Hey!" the desk sergeant snapped. "Dominguez! What do you think you're doing?"

"He was getting unruly," Dominguez replied.

"No, I wasn't! She just handcuffed me, and says she's going to take me into an interview room and..."

"Unlock him this instant!" The black officer stepped out from behind the counter.

"Jealous, Delouise?"

"Please Delouise, help me!" Jackson pled.

The black officer put her hand on her gun and unbuckled her holster. "Let him go, Domignuez."

"Why should I?!" Domignuez stood, her hand on the handle of *her* pistol.

The black officer woman locked eyes with Jackson and winked. "Cuz that piece of sweet white meat belongs to me."

Jackson's stomach twisted. "Oh God..."

"I saw him first, *perra gorda*!" Dominguez shouted, and drew her gun.

Almost as fast, the black officer woman drew her weapon, and Jackson had only enough time to throw himself—and his tethered chair—to the floor as the shots rang out. Dominguez fell only a few feet away, her sightless eyes staring at him.

Tears ran down Jackson's face, and he covered his head as male officers started shouting, followed by more gunshots and then the thud of another body hitting the floor.

————

J ackson sat on the cement steps in front of the police station. It was early, the sun having just crested the horizon. Some paramedic—a man—had placed a blanket around his shoulders, and despite the rapidly warming temperature, he shivered.

Two women had died fighting over *him!* This wasn't fun anymore. Jackson dug in his pocket and pulled out the black figurine of the woman. Could he destroy the talisman? Would that stop this madness?

A light blasting into his face made Jackson wince, and he turned his head and raised an arm to cover his face. "What the..."

"This is Axel Hendricks of KW80 Channel Seven, coming to you live from Southbridge Police Station where a shootout erupted between two officers."

Jackson uncovered his face and glanced up to find a man with a microphone standing in front of a man with a shoulder mounted camera.

"I stand here with one of the witnesses, Jackson Keller." The man stepped to the side so that the camera—and it's light—again focused on Jackson. "Tell us son, what did you see?"

Jackson stared at the reporter and stammered, "Th-they shot at each other. The one woman died, and the other was killed by the other cops."

"And do you know what caused the dispute that escalated so quickly into such bizarre violence?"

"Uh... me."

The reporter furrowed his brow. "What was that, son?"

"It was me. They were fighting over me."

"And why were they fighting over you?"

"They both wanted me. Like, in a sexual way."

An incredulous laugh escaped the reporter's lips, but he recovered quickly. "This is no joke, son. Two police officers are dead."

Before Jackson could answer, the camera man interrupted the reporter. He motioned to an earpiece. "Edison says the AP is picking up our coverage."

The reporter grinned, showing off immaculate white teeth. "Axel Hendricks, you handsome son of a gun, you've hit the big time!"

"Wait," Jackson said. "What does that mean?"

The reporter looked back down at him. "It means that your chubby face and story are going international."

An explosion of panic froze Jackson's chest. "No!"

"What's wrong, son?" the reporter asked. "Every news outlet on the planet is going to carry this story. Your homely face will be everywhere. You're gonna be famous, and I'm gonna be getting job offers."

"NO!" Jackson stood, dropping his blanket. He made a feeble attempt to grab the camera but was easily repelled by the camera man.

"What's your problem?!" the reporter said.

Jackson didn't answer. Instead he ran. A few police officers called out, but he was able to duck the police tape and dart into an alley. He dropped the figurine on the ground and stomped on it, but it did nothing to damage it. He glanced around and found a loose cinderblock, lifted it up and brought it down on the statue of the nude woman. The cement broke, not leaving a scratch on the figurine.

Jackson shook his head. There had to be a way to break the spell. Maybe if he just got rid of it! He scooped up the figurine and tossed it in a dumpster and ran out of the alley. He picked the direction he thought his house was in and ran until he was out of breath—a full forty seconds—and slowed to walking.

A maroon minivan slowed to match his pace, and a middle-aged woman rolled down the window to shout at him. "Hey stud, you need a ride?"

"NO!" Jackson screeched and banked right to run in between two houses.

It hadn't worked. The spell wasn't broken.

He ran through a backyard and climbed the fence separating it from an adjoining house's backyard. While balancing on the top, he tipped sideways and fell five feet to the ground. Sucking wind, he rolled onto his back, staring up at the morning sky. A face appeared in his vision, looking down at him and smiling. It was an old woman dressed in overalls and a gardening sun hat. She grinned and began to unbutton her overalls.

Jackson scurried up and ran until he emerged on the opposite side of the block. Where was he? He recognized the street. He jogged, refusing to give into fatigue this time and consequently tasted blood, until he reached one of the neighborhood's boardwalks. It was a shabby thing with mostly closed down boutiques, and... "The tattoo parlor!" Jackson blurted out.

He crossed the street and banged on the glass door.

When the witch didn't answer, he pulled on the door and it opened. Jackson rushed into the small shop and began shouting. "Hey! I need you to undo your spell! People are killing each other over me!"

No response.

Jackson moved past the counter and through the beaded curtain into the back room. It was empty. No occult items lining the shelves, no posters of tattoo designs on the walls, and no witch. The only thing in the room was a small obsidian statue of a nude woman with long hair placed on a table—as if it had been waiting for him.

Jackson backed through the beaded curtain, tripping over his feet but catching himself on the counter before he fell. He started at the sound of someone shouting from outside. He walked to the window and found a mob of women moving down the street, looking into doors and down alleys.

"I saw him go this way!" one shouted.

Jackson moved away from the window, but it was too late. A plump, short-haired woman pointed at him. "There he is!"

The mob of women rushed toward the tattoo parlor, shattering the glass of the door and window as they climbed over each other to get inside. Before he knew it, Jackson was being mobbed like a victim in a zombie movie.

———

Jouvart watched the mushroom cloud from a distance. It couldn't hurt him, but the woman's body he inhabited was a fragile thing. All the humans were fragile things, which would make the chaos and destruction he caused especially effective. Like a tiny pebble thrown to start an avalanche, Jouvart had put events into motion and it'd only taken a few months before the nations of the world—overthrown by groups of passionate women—fired warheads at each other.

Jouvart stared at the small obsidian figurine he held in his hand. He had succeeded in starting the apocalypse. Now Heaven and Hell could meet in battle on Earth. The dark lord would be pleased.

As the shockwave rushed toward him, Jouvart left his mortal vessel, relishing in her screams as the wave of fire consumed her.

JASON KING

Jason King wishes he was raised on a desert planet by his aunt and uncle and watched over by a mysterious old recluse, but his life is much duller than that. He supposes that's why he started making up stories. Born in Salt Lake City Utah, Jason grew up on a steady  diet of anime, science fiction, Dungeons and Dragons, JRPG's, and chocolate cake donuts. He got skinny and pretended not to be a nerd just long enough to get married and start a family. And although dismayed by the revelation that Jason was a geek, his wife stuck with him and they are now the proud parents of four beautiful children. Jason holds a bachelor's degree in I.T. Management and is currently the Internet Marketing Manager for a local bookstore chain, but he is determined to one day quit his "9 to 5" and write full-time. He is a proud anonymous member of the Space Balrogs troupe, and he speaks Labrador.

Thomas Destiny by Jason King and Jon Grundvig

Twelve-year-old Thomas doesn't have a dad and so hasn't done much of the camping-fishing thing. But this year he gets to go on his first week-long summer camp, and it's shaping up to be the epic adventure his friends promised it would be...that is until he accidentally releases a demon hidden in a cave behind a waterfall and gets hurled through a dimensional rift.

Lost in an alien world, Thomas pledges to find a powerful shard of creation for the mysterious Dreja (dr-ey-yuh) Lord, Arvek, in exchange for passage back to Earth. At his side are Bruno, a baby giant who eats just about anything and has ambitions to someday taste giraffe. The druid, a robed vagrant who's incessant lying, stealing, and reckless antics continually endanger Thomas and the others. The "Green Dude," an unintelligible shapeshifting blob disguised in a hat and sunglasses. And Darius, a young wizard warrior sworn to fight the growing threat of an ancient evil.

To achieve victory, Thomas and his party of would-be heroes will have to survive a forest infested with wraiths and zombies, scale a lava spewing mountain of fire, traverse a cursed desert, and face the greatest challenge of all: their own woeful incompetence, pointless infighting, and an A.D.D.-like tendency to stumble into unnecessary peril. It'll take more than magic, bravery, and sacrifice for this band of misfits to save the Cosmos—it'll take a miracle.

Check out Jason's Website:
www.authorjasonking.com

Find all of Jason's Planet-Crippling stories on Amazon:
amzn.to/2MqvfoV

Like Jason on Facebook:
www.facebook.com/jason.king.319452

Follow **@JasonKing1979** on Twitter:
twitter.com/JasonKing1979

I'M NO MARTYR

Craig Nybo

I'm like a symbol of a military agglomeration.
I'm like an emblem in the background of our charred
    out, broken pittance of a nation.
I'm like a prophet to the men and the women packing
    bludgeon.
But, I ain't no chieftain of the band.
As a harbinger of peace, I'm an injunction.

"With guns, we all can overcome," in spray paint, a
    graffito.
Those were my words on the wall of city hall back in
    old San Marino.
They've canonized and jargonized those words so plain
    and simple.
But I'm not the man they think I am, who can wash
    his hands in the sacred lavabo.

I just put another on the fire,
It's awry, the incredulity of life.
I am not a champion or a martyr.

It's a lie, this fiduciary right.

We take what weapons we can find from the torched
  out army depots.
We say our prayers every night in any building
  bolstered up with a steeple.
We have our mantras and our phrase, we have our
  watchwords and our signals.
But they're spreading like a fire 'cross the land and
  fighting them is seeming kind of futile.

I am just terror stricken,
Of this whole bleeding mess that's brewing.
I'm nothing but a chicken.
And if they ever trust me,
They'll learn that I am a poser, just a creton.

Window dressing, man.
That's all I am.

I just put another on the fire,
It's awry, the incredulity of life.
I am not a champion or a martyr.
It's a lie, this fiduciary right.

I just put another on the fire,
It's awry, the incredulity of life.
I am not a champion or a martyr.
It's a lie, this fiduciary right.

I just put another on the fire,
It's awry, the incredulity of life.
I am not a champion or a martyr.
It's a lie, this fiduciary right.

Well, it's time to get a life now.
Forget everything I said.
I ain't the one to lead you.
I ain't no arrowhead.
If you think I have a trick,
That I haven't shared,
You got another thing coming,
Another thing instead.

Get down.
Get down.
Get down.
I ain't no martyr, man.

————

Listen to Craig Nybo sing **I'm No Martyr***, free on YouTube:*
https://www.youtube.com/watch?v=MR5455qX-aQ

CRAIG NYBO

Craig Nybo lives with his beautiful wife and kids in Kaysville, UT. He works as a creative director for mediaRif.com, a digital agency. Craig writes novels, short fiction, and screenplays. Craig belongs

to an exclusive writers group called The Space Balrogs. With the Balrogs, he tours conventions and other events to perform theater-style panels with plenty of audience appeal. As a musician, he has released several records with friends under the band names Rustmonster and The Big Sky Country Boys. Craig also records solo work. He has released three records under his own name, Zombie Sing-a-long, and a sequel album, Zombie Sing-a-long: Whistler and the Children (Part 1). As a filmmaker, Craig has written and directed many short films. He also writes and directs many commercials and industrial videos as part of his profession. Aside from writing, Craig enjoys playing in the Rocky Mountains, rock climbing and canyoneering.

Dead Girl by Craig Nybo

A half-century-old curse lies over the small community of Ridgewater ever since Sarah Chase died in a car accident during a teen-angst-driven game of chicken back in 1962. She perished in the back seat of a 1961 Impala, accompanied by a group of boys who called themselves "the big four." She screamed as the car careened through a guardrail and plunged into the icy river water beneath. The four boys survived. Sarah did not.

Teenagers still race and party at the Milvian Bridge where Sarah's car went over, especially on the anniversary of her death, in hopes of catching a glimpse of her unsettled ghost.

But the partying teenagers of Ridgewater don't know that in life Sarah belonged to a group of teenage girls who practiced witchcraft. They don't now that Sarah seeks to use her powers from the grave to avenge her unrequited vendetta. They don't know that Stan Corelis, the driver of the Impala that terrible night and the unpronounced protector of Ridgewater, has passes away, freeing Sarah to unleash her anger.

Check out Craig's Website:
craignybo.com

Find all of Craig's Creep-tastic Books on Amazon:
amzn.to/2NawPrv

Like Craig on Facebook:
www.facebook.com/craig.nybo

Follow **@CraigNybo** on Twitter:
twitter.com/CraigNybo

DARK WINGS FROM ABOVE

Daniel Swenson

The alarm of the fire suppression system rang out as an explosion rocked the compound tossing Miguel Sanchez from his makeshift bunk. He hit the cold steel floor with a resounding thud. As he groaned in pain, he could hear the Master bellowing orders for everyone to get to their posts.

"Oh my god, they've found us," mumbled a scraggly wisp of a man not more then eighteen years old. "How? How could they have found us?" He fumbled with the laces on his boots.

Miguel, pulling himself up off the floor, could see that Harold was extremely frightened. "What's going on?" he asked.

The alarms chimed in Miguel's ears as another explosion rocked the compound, nearly knocking Miguel and Harold off their feet. Harold screamed out in panic as he raced out the door, forgetting his weapon and body armor. Miguel cursed and ran after the kid.

Hundreds of men and women cluttered the narrow metal and cement corridors of what was the last vestige of humanity. Miguel had been living there for a few months now after years of living a life on the run from the creatures that had come out of nowhere. Some had crawled out of the dark waters of the oceans, others out of tunnels and caverns deep beneath the earth. The most brilliant and devastating display had been those who had erupted, along with the ash and molten lava, from the volcanoes they'd been hiding in. A splendid way for all the world to see the arrival of the dragons.

These giant reptilian creatures were an unstoppable force that had destroyed city after city. Nothing survived when a nest of dragons descended from the skies.

Well that isn't entirely true, Miguel thought as he raced down the corridors. *I survived somehow.*

The compound was nothing more than a repurposed football stadium with a retractable roof that no longer worked. If Miguel remembered correctly, it used to be home to the Arizona Diamondbacks. Like Miguel, many of the people there sought shelter and some tangible reminder of their old lives. Living on the road, traveling from town to town, hadn't been difficult thanks to his military training. But over time Miguel had felt himself slowly slipping into madness out there on his own.

It was because of his military background he'd been given the small platoon of fifteen young men by the master sergeant. The men ranged in age from eighteen to twenty-four. None of them had any previous training other than what they had been forced to learn out in the wilds that remained of the world. The master sergeant hoped Miguel could mold them into some semblance of defenders. Unfortunately, one by one he'd lost them. The first to perish was Nathaniel. Nathaniel had witnessed too much loss and devastation in his short twenty-two years. Even though life at the compound was so much better than that out on the road, the young man had taken his life. The remainder of the platoon he'd lost to accidents, the harsh reality of this life, the dragons, or just sheer stupidity. All that remained was Harold.

A small boy about nine or ten darted out in front of Miguel causing him to nearly trip over the boy as he ran past trying to catch up to Harold. He cursed as the boy toppled over, skinning his knee. He began to wail. His mother quickly ran over and scooped him up, offering her apology. Miguel smiled and nodded. He understood all too well the pains of being a parent to a rambunctious ten-year-old.

"The demons are here!" Harold shouted. "Say farewell to your loved ones!"

Miguel could see the fear on everyone's faces. Another explosion from up above rattled the metal pipes that ran along the corridor causing everyone around Miguel to cry out. Fear was ever present in everyday life now. You never knew what day would be your last or if it would bring about the death of a loved one.

The last thing any of these people need is Harold's mad ramblings, Miguel thought to himself.

Miguel continued to wade through the sea of frightened people, trying to catch up with Harold. Shortly after Harold had arrived with the last caravan from the wilds, Miguel had mentioned to the master sergeant that it was obvious the kid had suffered some pretty nasty trauma. The grumpy commander just grunted and told Miguel that was his problem.

"*Maldicion!*" Miguel cursed as he exited the corridor and realized he'd lost sight of Harold.

He ran down the corridor and up several flights of stairs searching for any sign of the young man. The rattle of automatic gunfire and the boom of the anti-tank cannons mixed with the screams of the dying and the roar of the unearthly beasts. Annoyed, Miguel fired his gun at the alarm speaker, causing a couple of individuals in the corridor to spin around with guns at the ready.

Shaking his head at his own foolishness, Miguel slowly holstered his gun and held his hands up high. Realizing he wasn't a threat, the others quickly ran off to wherever they'd been heading. Miguel breathed out a small sigh of relief. The ceiling above him rattled as something large slammed into the grandstands above. Several small cracks ran along the cement pillars that held the ceiling aloft. Unsure how much longer the ceiling would remain, he scampered off toward a nearby door that was slightly ajar, fearing Harold had been shortsighted enough to race outside.

As Miguel approached the door he pulled his side arm as he wasn't sure what state of mind the poor fool would be in when he caught up to him. There was a sudden shift in air pressure as he reached the door, something inside him cried out a warning, and Miguel dove to the side seconds before the door blasted inward, tearing itself free from its hinges. The large metal door whistled past like a missile and slammed into the wall opposite Miguel. Dust and debris cascaded down causing him to cough and choke on the air in the corridor. When the air finally cleared enough for him to see, Miguel whispered a small prayer of gratitude. On the other side of the corridor, the door was imbedded seven or eight inches deep into the concrete wall.

Flames danced here and there in the debris as Miguel rose. The electrical system buzzed as it tried to kick on the fire suppression system. A flash of electricity arced from a damaged power conduit, and the lights winked out. The large anti-tank cannon above him went silent.

"Oh no!" he muttered. *Without the cannon, they'll never be able to keep the dragons from making it down to the field.*

"They're here..." Harold's voice sounded just outside the door. "The aberrations of hell have finally come. All the major cities have been destroyed. Why did I think this place would be any different...?"

Miguel was amazed that he had heard Harold's crazed mumbling over the chaos of the battle that raged on outside. The overwhelming noises, the intense Arizona heat, and his own fears threatened to overwhelm his senses. Knowing that Harold was in danger, Miguel shielded his eyes from the harsh glare of the sunlight and slowly approached the door. Unsure what he'd find beyond the threshold, Miguel took a deep breath and darted outside as fast as his feet could carry him.

Something large hit the ground behind him. The thick-scaled, club-like tail of a dragon tore towards Miguel. He dove to the side, tumbling behind the broken and twisted remains of what used to be the compound's helicopter. The creature's tail struck what was left of the helicopter with such force that it caused the wreckage to soar across the open expanse of the old football field. It crashed into the west bleachers, destroying another of the anti-tank cannons and killing several of the people manning it.

The dragon bellowed in triumph as more of its kind descended down through the broken retractable ceiling. Miguel calmly crept away from the winged creature. The hellish monster swiveled its head, turning its cruel gaze toward him. A wave of fear rolled over Miguel. He froze. Try as he might, he couldn't get his legs to respond to his mental commands. The hot Arizona sun enveloped him, yet ice coursed through his veins. The last time he'd seen eyes like that—his entire family had died.

He, his wife, and two boys had gone over to his sister-in-law's house to celebrate his niece's twelfth birthday. The backyard had been strung up with lights. His father-in-law was busy at the grill roasting meats, several of his nephews and brother-in-laws were busy playing instruments while merrily singing. A piñata hung from one of the three Rocky Mountain white oak trees that stood in their back yard.

They celebrated another year of his niece's presence in their lives. They ate cake and ice cream and joked with one another. It had been a wonderful night where he had danced with his wife, chased after his ten and twelve-year-old sons, and made an utter fool of himself trying to sing Ritchie Valen's 'La Bamba'. The dark winged creatures descended out of the skies and that one perfect moment was snuffed out like the flames of the birthday candles.

The familiar thumping of several grenade launchers brought Miguel out of his reveries. He turned and ran as the small fist-sized projectiles exploded upon impact, blasting away huge patches of the creature's scaly hide. The shock-wave threw Miguel off his feet and slammed him into a wall of sand bags. The dragon's screams of pain were deafening and caused Miguel's ears to bleed.

Miguel looked up to find Harold standing on the other side of the sandbag wall clutching a Bible in his hands. "When the Lamb opened the second seal, I heard the second living creature say, 'Come!' Then another horse came out, a fiery one. Its rider given power to take peace from the earth and to make people kill one another..."

From out of nowhere, a small dragon swooped down and snatched Harold up in its razor-sharp talons. Blood sprayed the sand bags and Miguel's face and as quickly as the dragon had attacked, both it and the eighteen-year-old boy were gone. The only proof that Harold had been there was the torn and blood stained bible that he'd been holding.

The remaining anti-tank cannons fired off in rapid succession, blasting the life out of the reptilian creatures that were foolish enough to squeeze their way through the broken retractable roof. The concussions of the cannons echoed across the expanse of the neglected sports stadium causing Miguel to slam his hands over his ears. Blood drizzled from his nose and ears as the shock wave rolled through him.

Where can I best help the other defenders? he thought.

Chaos and death reigned down upon the defenders as more of the creatures fought their way into the open expanse of the football field. Miguel ran toward a nearby chain gun. He dodged past portions of debris that came crashing down from the ceiling above. Several of the smaller dragons dodged their way through the falling debris and the devastating blasts from the anti-tank cannons and chain guns. They began picking off one defender after another.

One of the smaller serpents feasting on its latest victim noticed Miguel running. The foul creature screeched before it leaped into the air using its wings to gain altitude. When the creature reached the height it wanted, it snapped in its wings and plummeted towards Miguel like a speeding bullet.

Miguel saw the creature hurtling toward him out of the corner of his eye. He turned and fired several rounds from his side arm toward the creature as he did his best to keep running. The bullets glanced off the creature's thick scales.

"Damn it!" Miguel threw the useless pistol and redoubled his efforts to get to the chain gun.

The serpent hissed in excitement as it opened its wings. The wings scooped up the air, instantly pulling the creature back as it reached out with all four of its limbs tipped with razor-sharp talons toward Miguel's back. Miguel dove forward, launching himself head first over the wall of sand bags barely avoiding the deathly grasp of the smaller and lither serpent as it swished past overhead screaming in rage about its lost prey.

Miguel tumbled across the hard ground, afraid to stand and have that creature snatch him up like poor Harold. Miguel crawled on all fours over to the Tesla generator that powered the chain gun. He flipped the switch on the generator causing the motor on the chain gun to whine as it spun. The sky directly above him clear, he jumped to his feet, flipped off the safety, and unleashed a devastating blazing barrage of hell upon the flying reptiles.

"*Mueren ustedes, hijos de puta escamosos!*" he cursed as he continued to fire upon the flying serpents.

The light-weight thirty millimeter rounds tore through the smaller dragons as if they were nothing more than over-bloated flying swine. Blood and gore sprayed the benches of the northwest corner of the stadium as Miguel unloaded the entire belt full of rounds. Pain and rage bubbled up inside Miguel as he stood there whipping the chain gun back and forth, killing serpent after serpent. He had bottled up the pain of losing his wife and two sons to these damn creatures long ago. But now it came rushing to the surface, and he wove a tapestry of obscenities that would have made any sailor blush.

"Hold up!" Someone shouted over the PA system that still amazingly worked. "I think that's the last of them."

Miguel breathed a sigh of relief. It appeared as if the dragons had retreated.

Could it be possible that we've finally won a battle against these monstrosities? he wondered.

Something big slammed into the northern wall just above the nosebleed seats. The entire stadium rattled from the impact. Miguel looked up as three colossal dragons burst through the wall creating a gigantic breach that allowed more of the creatures to surge through in a massive swarm of death.

It didn't take long for nightmarish creatures to rip, bite, and tear their way through the defense up on the northern wall. The initial breach had taken out several of the chain gun placements up there along with the brave men and women that stood their ground and valiantly fought against the oncoming horde.

Miguel stood transfixed, mesmerized by the brutal display of carnage unfolding up on the wall. Something in the back of his mind screamed out for him to run away and never look back. But he couldn't. He stood there frozen as if the creatures had cast some sort of holding spell upon him. Despair settled over him as one of the colossal dragons slammed its meaty, clawed hand down upon one of the anti-tank cannons, smashing it into oblivion.

"We can't win," he mumbled. "Harold was right. They've come for us."

Trembling, Miguel stumbled back and plopped down on the sandbags. Sweat stung his eyes as he wiped his face with his blood stained shirt.

I should have bolted like Harold did after the first explosion rocked the compound, stolen a truck and gotten the hell out of here. He shuddered. *There's no chance of that happening now. We're doomed.*

He watched as the last two remaining anti-tank cannons swiveled around and began firing on the colossal dragons. The bombardment slammed into the creatures, followed by a series of massive explosions—like several fists of orange flame had blasted their way into the swarm of reptiles from some god of fire. Miguel had never seen anything like it. A deadly rainfall consisting of thousands of pieces of concrete and steel showered down around Miguel and the other defenders. A small part of Miguel began to rise up feeling some semblance of hope that they had possibly finally destroyed the colossal beasts and the swarm that had come to annihilate them.

A cry pierced the air above the roar of flames. It sounded like a mountain had been pushed over the edge of a cliff to go rebounding down the cliff face to the ground below. The sound was so harsh that the hairs on the back of Miguel's neck stood up on end as if someone had run their nails down the surface of a chalkboard.

"Miguel watch out!" Someone shouted.

One of the larger dragons hit the ground near Miguel, pelting him with chunks of dirt and debris. Miguel cried out and toppled over backwards. The act saved his life as the creature's tail came crashing down, crushing the chain gun and the sand bags where he'd been sitting. The bloated body of the creature twisted and turned as it tried to right itself, narrowly missing his prone form. The audible snap of the creature's wings echoed in Miguel's ear as he laid there in a daze upon the ground. The serpent's screech of pain brought Miguel out of his stupor.

He quickly assessed the situation around him and struggled to get to his feet, fighting to get his air back. His stomach lurched, threatening to expel its contents, but he managed to straighten up. Insanity raged all around him. Men and women were dying by the dozens. The younger, smaller dragons littered the ground of the stadium. But the bigger, stronger creatures were decimating the humans.

Miguel's eyes narrowed on the injured beast that thrashed about not too far away from home. Rage flashed across Miguel's face. He heard the sweet melody of his beautiful wife's voice, the laughter of his two boys, and the hammering of his own heart.

The creature suffered greatly, most likely near death from the giant gaping hole in its side. Blood gushed freely from the garish wound. Miguel could only assume that the beast had been hit by one of the anti-tank cannons as the serpent's scales and soft tissue had been blasted away by something powerful. Now all that remained was damaged tissue, blood, and the bones that were keeping the creature's internal organs from spilling out all over the ground.

Miguel smiled as his eyes settled upon a jagged piece of

steel that lay upon the ground. He wasn't sure how it'd got there, but it was an answer to his unspoken prayers. He may not survive today's onslaught, but at least he'd be the one responsible for taking out one of the larger and more threatening dragons.

If I'm lucky it will be one of the females, he thought as he snatched up the piece of steel and charged.

The creature was completely unaware of him as he came racing in. He leapt over the creature's tail as it swept towards him in the beast's thrashing. He ducked under one of the creature's taloned legs as it raked the air. He could see his target now. A small corner of the dragon's heart appeared past the edge of the open wound with each beat. A shadow passed over Miguel as he neared the wounded creature. He raised his makeshift sword, prepared to strike the wounded serpent, when something struck him from behind.

Miguel's body arched backward, his unprotected head whipped back, all of his momentum snapping back on him like a broken rubber band. He lifted right up off his toes, clearing the ground. For one long moment his body hung suspended in the air. Then he landed with a thud.

Dazed fury colored Miguel's vision red. Everything around him blurred as he lay upon the ground, pain running up every nerve in his back. Something strong hit him in the chest, blasting the air from his lungs with a groan and driving him further into the ground. A second dragon's toothy maw hovered overhead. The smell of the creature's hot carrion-scented breath made the bile in his stomach churn and threatened to make its way up his throat. Pure hatred glimmered in both Miguel's and the creature's eyes as they met. Large beads of saliva dribbled from the beast's razor sharp teeth, splattering Miguel's face and chest.

One of the serpent's talons had pierced through Miguel's body armor, digging into his flesh. His mind screamed out as the pain drove through his shoulder and into his back. His thoughts became confused as the burning pain licked down his back like a scorching fire. His face scrunched up in a grimace as tears streamed down his face. People around him screamed, shouted and died. Anger swept through him at the chaos and pain—pain for those around him that he wanted to protect but couldn't. Pain for the loss of his wife and children. Pain at the loss of a potential future with them that would never come.

"Do it!" Miguel grunted. "Come on, you son of a bitch, you've got me. Just do it!"

He slammed his fists futilely against the creature's thick scaly claws. The dragon gave a low throaty chortle as if his weak attempts to free himself amused it. Miguel watched in detached horror as the dragon's amusement washed away in an instant, and the creature's head snapped forward to end Miguel's life.

And so this is how it ends, he thought as he closed his eyes.

ime seemed to slow down in that instant as a loud explosion stole Miguel's hearing. Something large thumped to the ground next to him, his pain intensified as the beast's talon ripped free of his shoulder, the pressure on his chest eased, and he suddenly found himself being bathed in a fountain of warm and sticky fluid.

He opened his eyes. He was covered head to toe in the dragon's blood. Its headless corpse lay next to him, and a shower of blood erupted from its tattered and torn neck. Miguel knelt down and snatched up the jagged piece of steal he'd been holding earlier. He stalked over to the body of the wounded dragon that lay weakly thrashing just a few feet away. Pain thrummed throughout his whole body. He knew at least one or two ribs were broken, but he used that pain to guide him on.

Anger as hot as lava boiled within him, fueling his limbs.

It churched within, hungry for destruction as he raised the steel blade. The pressure of the raging sea of anger inside demanded action. He screamed something incoherent as he jammed the jagged steel deep into the dying dragon's heart.

An unearthly wail shattered the chaos around him.

The dragon's body thrashed about wildly in protest to its heart suddenly stopping. Too weak to move, Miguel smiled in satisfaction as one of the creature's legs struck him in the chest, sending him flying through the air to slam into the wall behind him. The pain that once burned like fire faded away into an icy numbness. Black filled the edges of his vision as his breath came in ragged, shallow gasps.

"Mia my sweet, it finally looks like I'll be joining you and the boys," he whispered as the darkness swallowed him.

———

The atmosphere was dead and dry as Miguel slowly opened his eyes. Darkness drizzled the sky, melting away all color and consuming the light. His body ached and his head throbbed as if someone had been hammering away at it for hours while he lay unconscious. All around him was death. The stadium lay quiet, for it was now a graveyard of the unburied. The corpses of both human and dragon lay scattered across the open field and the remains of the stadium's seating. They lay like dolls over the ground, limbs at awkward angles and heads held in such a way that they could not be only sleeping. Nothing more than abandoned shells left to rot out in the open.

The wind moaned through the broken remains of the building as the light began to disappear. The whole scene reeked of melancholy and emptiness. There was a quick flicker and crackle of light, too fast for the naked eye. Suddenly the soft warm glow of a firefly sliced through the dark atmosphere with its sugary light. It buzzed through the blackened air, a gentle illuminating sun which ate away at the darkness before it zipped away.

Miguel sighed as he realized death had escaped him once again. Silence hung in the air like the suspended moment before a falling piece of glass shattered on the ground. The silence was a gaping void, needing to be filled with sounds, words, anything.

"How long have I been out?" Miguel groaned, breaking the silence.

His muscles felt weak, just like his energy. He let out an exasperated sigh, groaning as he rolled to his side. Many questions shot through his mind as he tried to get his feet underneath him. Aside from his own noisy breath, there was nothing to be heard. Miguel rummaged through his pockets and found the small LED flashlight he'd been searching for. He clicked the button on the bottom, and light illuminated the area around him.

Miguel's jaw tightened. Fire in the form of tears stung his nut-brown eyes, threatening their attack. He crunched his teeth over his lip. Salty blood filled his mouth. Slowly, Miguel picked up his feet in an unbalanced gait, carelessly dropping the lead weights to the ground with each harrowing step toward the hole in the wall he'd chased Harold out of.

Reality tried to tap its way into his brain--everyone was dead. He was the only one out of the two thousand people that lived there left alive. He knew no one had escaped the wrath of the demonic horde of serpents. Step by agonizing step he made the long way up to the announcer's box. He knew there was radio equipment up there he could use to send out a transmission.

Nausea swirled unrestrained in Miguel's empty stomach. His head swam with half-formed regrets. His blood became like tar as his heart struggled to keep a steady beat. Miguel's melancholy mood hung over him like a black cloud, raining personal sorrow down upon him. He reached the announcer's box, found the radio, and whispered a prayer as flipped the switch on the Tesla generator that powered it.

His heartbeat echoed in his ears like guards of honor firing a salute at a funeral—a grim reminder of his own mortality. It beat so loud that it seemed to want to escape his chest. He didn't dare move, didn't dare breathe; he remained frozen as he waited on baited breath for the radio to respond. His heart pounded in his chest... *duh-duhn, duh-duhn.* The hairs on his arms stood at attention, as a militia of chills marched down his spine.

The radio flickered to life, bathing the room with the orange glow of its light. Miguel sighed in relief as he sat down in the chair next to it. The sound of static filled the room as he adjusted the settings on the device. When he found the channel he was looking for, he pulled the microphone close and pressed the transmission button.

"My name is Miguel Sanchez. To anyone still alive listening to this broadcast I say, I hope that somehow you and the rest of humanity will somehow survive. That you will find someway to overcome the pestilence of the dragons that ravage our world. Life as you know it has become far different than that of what we once knew. No one knows where these things came from, but I do know they seek for our utter and complete destruction. I beg you to survive and find a way to climb up out of these earthen prisons we ourselves have created. Learn from our mistakes and make this world a better place than it was before these creatures came. Find a way to live in peace and know that there is something far worse in this world than warring amongst ourselves..."

Something dark slunk its way into the announcer booth behind Miguel. The orange glow of the radio's light reflected off its dark obsidian colored scales like a thousand tiny shards of glass. The serpent's long sinuous neck lifted its head above Miguel's unknowing form.

"I don't know if any of us will make it out of this battle against the dragons alive, but if we do I hope to find you on the other...."

Miguel's blood curdled scream pierced the darkness, echoing across the corpse-filled stadium, before falling into eerie silence.

Glass exploded out from the announcer booth as the inky black form of the dragon burst through the exterior of the booth, lifting itself high into the night sky on its powerful diaphanous wings. The creature's crimson orbs reflected the cold glare of the moon above as it rose above the broken remains of the stadium.

Flames erupted from its open maw, bathing the roof of the stadium in flames. The power of the creature's breath melted both metal and concrete alike; causing what was left of the building to collapse in upon itself. When it was satisfied, it closed its mouth, extinguishing the deluge of flames.

The creature smiled in satisfaction, bellowing a triumphant cry as more of its kind appeared around it. The creatures sniffed at the air, relishing in the smell of burning flesh. One by one the serpents bowed their heads in reverence to the larger dragon. Avarice showed in the obsidian scaled dragon's crimson eyes as it turned its bulky body toward the east, pumping its wings as it flew off into the night sky above its new kingdom.

DANIEL SWENSON

Daniel Swenson lives with his wife and children in Utah, nestled between the foothills of the mountains and the shore of Utah Lake. He and his family enjoy hiking, riding bikes, playing  outdoors and game nights where they play different board and card games.

Daniel has been a fan of science fiction and fantasy since he first sat down and watched Star Wars, Voltron, Masters of the Universe and the Transformers. Since witnessing the spectacle of Star Wars, Daniel has been an avid movie goer. He found his love of reading at a young age when he journeyed in the lands of Krynn and Toril alongside the creations of R.A. Salvatore, Margaret Weis and Tracy Hickman.

He is the creator and host of the Hugo-nominated podcast Dungeon Crawlers Radio, a successful podcast that covers all things geek including interviews with upcoming and best-selling authors. Because of the show, Daniel has been able to build relationships among the writing and publishing community that has helped to cultivate his talents.

The Shadow Above the Flames by Daniel Swenson

How do you save the world from two monstrous entities? A power-hungry corporation and a newly awakened dragon...

In a world left reeling at the loss of fossil fuels, and after giving years of service to the military, Henry Morgan just wants a normal life. But between nagging feelings from his past and a strained rela-

tionship with his brother Rick, "normality" always feels just out of reach.

The Union Forest Corporation puts profits ahead of safety and with a dragon on the loose threatening to kill innocent people, something incredible happens...

Henry learns that Rick is among the force of elite commandos sent by Union Forest to battle against the dragon at the drilling site, he's forced back into the roles of soldier and protective older sibling. He'll do anything he can to save his brother . . . including risking his own life at the hands of a ruthless corporation. Henry may be the only person who can keep the world safe from total annihilation.

Check out Daniel's Website:
www.dragonsfate.com

Find all of Daniel's Ground-Burning Books on Amazon:
amzn.to/2MJYVwQ

Like Daniel on Facebook:
www.facebook.com/daniel.swenson.96

Follow **@DanielSwenson77** on Twitter:
twitter.com/DanielSwenson77

DOG WILL HUNT

David J. West

The curtain of night fell, and as the pinprick of stars began to pierce, a metallic silver airship reeled downward and disappeared over the range of cactus laden hills. The sound of squealing thunder broke, and the tremors of the impact made the cattle stampede.

Rogers assumed the airship to be some contraption that scientist inventor folks back east made, but a vile stink on the wind gave him pause. Following the foul reek, Rogers pondered what cargo could smell so horrible. But curiosity was stronger than his stomach.

The horse shied from venturing closer, and it took all his savage skills to keep the mount moving. Faint crackles and flickering lights like a drunken Christmas teased on the other side of the hills, and Rogers thought he heard metal tearing.

He kicked the flanks of his mount and galloped closer, but at the top of the last hill, Rogers's horse bucked him off and fled. Cursing the animal, he was astounded by what he saw from the ridgeline.

A deep furrow plowed through the hillside as the airship

lay crippled a quarter-mile distant. Green flames illuminated the crash. Rogers had never seen anything so large.

He wondered why he heard no cry of pain or fear, no sound of anything living or even dying.

Marveling at the vastness, Rogers pondered how such a thing could fly. It appeared to be entirely metal, but how could such a thing even get off the ground? It was more like a sky ship than a balloon air-ship. This defied every bit of common sense he knew.

Rogers had fought in the war and was an experienced rancher, he saw life and death nearly every other day out here on the open range and amidst the stench of noxious fuel, he also caught the stink of offal from dead bodies. He pulled out his revolver and stepped inside through a gaping hole.

The constant crackling and sparking from broken nodes along the wall granted just enough light to see. He looked at the wires hanging limp like roots in a cave and puzzled at their function. Telegraph wires inside an airship? There was a slim amount of writing on the walls here and there, but it wasn't English and though Rogers was barely literate in Spanish, he knew it wasn't either tongue.

Then Rogers saw the first one.

A hand lay palm up. It belonged to a man.

Rogers went to feel for a pulse but stopped when he saw a pool of red and realized that something had been chewing on him. The man's legs were almost gone, and what was left had ghastly teeth marks.

Flinching backward, Rogers scanned the gloom. Was the stink of death even stronger now?

Shadows danced, and he glanced about warily, sure something stirred in that gloomy crypt of a ship.

He paused for the longest ten seconds of his life before he stood and moved, gun barrel forward, further exploring the death ship.

In what looked to be a wheelhouse with curious dials and switches, two more men lay sprawled out. Their mouths hung open as if they had died screaming. There were bite marks here too, their necks were twisted at unnatural angles it looked as if this had done them in instead of something hungering. Dull black mirrors, cracked and useless, were affixed to the walls, and Rogers couldn't understand their use. If this was the wheelhouse, how could a pilot navigate? He couldn't even see outside.

Down the shadowy hallway, Rogers caught sight of a door that had been smashed off its hinges. A look in revealed a small room with several cots and a privy. Long thick cables embedded in the wall connected to multiple pairs of manacles. They had been snapped.

"Sons of bitches escaped," he muttered aloud to himself.

Rogers found over a dozen more dead littered about the ship, left like corn husk dolls abandoned for a better prize around every new corner. Most had been chewed on and a number had been torn apart. Such strength in close quarters seemed impossible, but this airship was unbelievable, why should anything else seem ridiculous now?

Traveling back through the wheelhouse, Rogers looked again for an atlas or log to grant him a glimpse of a way to better understand this strange airship. He found a slim rectangle that resembled a book. A latch let the thing flip open. Curious characters presented themselves on half of its face while the other side had a dark mirror similar to those on the walls. Rogers ran his hand across the smooth surface, and the blank face fired to life.

A portrait of a man appeared and began speaking.

Rogers nearly dropped the devilish device.

The portrait stumbled out a frantic, nonsensical language, which almost sounded like Spanish but didn't have any of the familiar words. The voice changed timbre and speech a half-dozen times then finally addressed Rogers in a serviceable English. "Why are you aboard our ship? Where is my crew? Are the Apophis still contained?"

Rogers didn't answer at first but pulled a flask of whiskey from his coat and took a long pull, never taking his eyes off the portrait.

The portrait waited.

Rogers looked around the room. "You talking to me?"

"Yes."

Another swallow.

"You must answer me. Where is my crew?"

Roger's wiped his beard with his sleeve. "Dead."

"Everyone?"

"Near as I can tell, they're all goners."

"What of the Apophis? Are they still contained?"

"Don't know what that is, but if you're asking about the prisoners, they've escaped. Looks like they took to a bit of cannibalism to boot. Don't worry, we'll catch them. The law out here is mighty handy." Rogers opened his coat and tapped a dented tin star that hung there.

"The Apophis are not men. You should seek shelter as best you can. A Colonial recovery team is on its way, but it may not get to your world for some time."

Frowning, Rogers muttered, "My world? What the hell, you talking 'bout?"

"You should hide; keep out of sight of the Apophis. My apologies to your world for the destruction they shall wreak."

"What're they gonna do?"

"They bring chaos. Death."

Roger's squinted at the portrait. "I've taken down the worst men from Yuma to Galveston, ain't no man I'm a'feared of."

"The Apophis are not men."

"You tried to contain 'em like one."

The portrait snapped, "I warn you, primitive, for your own sake stay out of this."

The mirror faded to black, and Rogers puzzled at this display. He was angered at the portrait's dismissal of his skills. If there was a lawman who had taken down more outlaws, Rogers hadn't heard of them. His reputation was legendary, though vilified by some. He was usually humble about it too, until he was completely dismissed like that. Now he had something to prove to the haughty foreigner. And the black mirror—this was an invention that left the telegraph in the dust of ages. Men were polite on the telegraph, perhaps the dark mirror made men rude, and that ain't worth a damn.

Something shambled toward Rogers in the dark.

He cocked his gun as the shadow grew.

Rasping, ragged breath let Rogers know this was not the enemy but a panting survivor of the crash. A silver-haired man dragged himself forward, and Rogers helped him lean against the wall. He was covered in bruises and wore a blood-stained jumpsuit. It was the queerest thing Rogers had ever seen a man wear.

"Let's take look at your wounds, pardner."

The man nodded and signaled for water but then passed out. Rogers no longer had his canteen but assumed there must be some stores somewhere on the airship for water or perhaps some whiskey. He gently laid the man down and got up to search through the wreckage again.

Opening a variety of panels and shelves in what might have been closets produced nothing, and Roger's was just about to give up on finding water when his hand ran beside a curious spout that shot out a blast of cool water. He didn't see a pump anywhere and looked above the stem and saw nothing. "Must be coming from the wall?" he said aloud, scratching his beard. He slapped the stem a few more times to no avail. He grabbed at it and pulled, and finally another blast of water shot out, surprising him. After a few tries, he discovered its sensitivity to his hand placement. He smiled, though still puzzling at this bizarre way of getting water. He filled up the sink then filled a cup for the silver suited man.

"I found some water, mighty curious contraption you have there," he said.

He had company.

A gaunt grey creature stood over the silver-haired man. It was short but had lean taut muscles and huge black eyes. Its small mouth gaped open, revealing tiny razors of teeth.

"I'll be dipped," mouthed Rogers.

The creature leapt, its dark claws dripping gore. A horrid screech preceded it.

Rogers drew his six-gun and blasted the thing. Bullets tore through its mottled hide and blue blood splashed the panels beyond. It screamed in agony while still clawing at Rogers who let loose a slew of profanity while emptying his gun. The monster hit the deck and, though gravely wounded, it still crawled at Rogers, scraping its claws vainly upon the steel deck, its bloody mouth opening and closing in jagged breath.

Taking a chunk of the steel panel that had been knocked loose from the wall, Rogers bashed the thing over the head until its black brains oozed out.

The silver-haired man was awake and slumped up against the wall. Rogers looked to him and shouted, "What the hell was that?"

The man shook his head, then touched a button on his suit and answered, "Say that again?"

"What the hell was that thing? A demon?"

"You could say that. The Apophis plague the known universe. These fourteen meant for a purgatory facility beneath your western ocean. Down in the deep trench beside what you call Catalina Island."

Rogers was sure the silver-haired man was insane, he could

not conceive of what had just been said, though all the words were in perfect English—yet what they suggested was madness.

"Come again?"

"Did you see any more nearby?"

"What? There are more of those things?" Rogers asked, as he reloaded.

"The Apophis. There should be at least thirteen more."

Rogers was painfully aware that he didn't have enough ammunition. The saddle bags on his fleeing horse had all his spare cartridges. His belt only held perhaps thirty rounds, and this monster had taken all six shots and had still been coming until he had clubbed its brains out.

"Do you have any guns?"

The silver-haired man looked at Rogers and shook his head. "Nothing like your primitive tool, no."

"What do you do to handle those things?"

"We capture them using Sonics and retire them to purgatory facilities far away from anything they can harm. If they escaped from the undersea prisons, they would be crushed by the depths and drown."

"But what about when they fight back, like just now? How do you kill them?"

"We do not kill, that would violate universal law."

"They seem ready enough to do unto you."

The silver-haired man was puzzled at Rogers's words. "They are outlaws," he said, struggling in vain to stand. "But we do not stoop to their abominable level."

"Here, I got you some water from that wacko stem," said Rogers, handing him the cup, before realizing it was empty from shooting at the creature. "I'll get you some more. But you gotta tell me what else you've got to deal with those things."

"We render them unconscious with sonic rays, once we

have determined that they are indeed outlaws. We do not kill, that is inhumane."

Rogers chuckled at that, it was the most foolish thing he had heard in a long time. That is, if it was even true. Perhaps it was a dream from too much whiskey, too much time in the sun the day before, maybe he had been bucked off and hit his head on a rock, and this would be over soon enough. But upon pinching himself, Rogers determined he was awake in the craziest stupor of his life. "So, tell me, how do you determine a monster is being an outlaw? Seems that kinda beast would always be that way."

"They aren't when they are born, but as they mature they do become... aggressive."

Rogers scoffed. "Would be a whole lot easier if you just exterminated them don'tcha think? Save a whole lotta headache. And heartache."

"We are not base animals. There is only one planet that has such wild and rebellious attitudes such as that."

"Lemme guess... this one?" Rogers swayed his arms wide.

"Quite. You would be surprised to learn that while there are dozens of civilizations that roam the nearby galaxy, few enough come here because of how incredibly violent your kind is. Yours is the only planet that actively kills."

"Ha! Good! What would we need with more weirdos visiting like this? And my kind? You look human enough."

"I am the same kind as you I suppose, but we do not drop to the indignity of murder."

Rogers shook his head. "In my experience, sometimes it needs to be done for the greater good."

"And for my soul I should rather die than kill another creature. It is not for me to take that right away from them."

Rogers spit. "That damn Apophis thing there, he seemed just fine with taking us both out. Hell, didn't it kill the rest of your crew here?"

The silver-haired man nodded. "And they will kill more of your fellow men as soon as they can find them. The more they find and feed the more of them that it will produce until they overwhelm entire populations. The nearest settlement will be in danger first. Do you know how many more escaped?"

"Awww shit. They all escaped, and my ranch is the nearest settlement." Rogers turned to the corridor. "I gotta get going. I ain't got much ammo, but I ain't gonna let those bastards touch anybody either."

"I do not condone your mission."

"Sure, sure. Anything else you can say to help me out?"

"No."

"Look, you guys crashed here and gave us a pickle we ain't never had. You owe me!"

The silver-haired man looked down. "You're right. This is our mistake. You pierced the Apophis many times in the body. Aim for the head."

"You don't have a sonic Air-Ray for me?"

The silver-haired man shook his head. "No. Go with god since I cannot."

"Uh huh. Dog will hunt."

Rogers stalked out of the ruin and looked at the ground, trying to see what he had missed earlier. Dozens of small webbed footprints littered the ground. He hadn't noticed them before because they were so alien to his usual senses, especially in light of this wreck. After all, a man can only see what he expects to see, you wouldn't notice something that never existed before if it wasn't drawing attention to itself, or would you? The prints circled the airship then banded together heading due west. At least it was away from his ranch, but it was heading toward the town of Andrewsville.

"I better get moving."

———

Dawn rose a little too red for Rogers's comfort. He had been hotfooting it as fast as his boots could carry him. He was mighty sore and tired, but he didn't let up one bit. Many a rustler had called him a relentless hound over the years, and these damn otherworldly monsters were about to taste his justice. How he wished he had his horse.

Then he found it. What was left of it.

Viciously mauled, it lay prone on the ground. Blood splashed over the mesquite and anthills. Rogers took off his hat and wiped his brow. At least he could get his ammo from the saddlebags. As he reached down, the torn gory body jerked and heaved.

Aghast, Rogers stepped back as a spiky head with glaring black eyes emerged from the ribcage! The monstrous Apophis had been gorging itself on the entrails.

Barely containing his rage and disgust Rogers emptied his revolver into the glaring dark eyes of the monster. It had time for one gruesome howl before lead silenced it forever.

"Ten left."

Though he had quickly dispatched the monster, one thing about the encounter worried Rogers. It had changed somewhat from the first one he had killed. This one was larger, both in the head and long sinewy clawed arms. It was taking on a different color too despite the bloody mess. Its mouth was also larger and seemed to distend when it roared at him. How much more would these things change?

Then he saw a clutch of eggs, pooled around the horse's belly. They were translucent, and he could see things inside swimming like tadpoles, but these were already as large as frogs. If he didn't destroy them an apocalypse would surely cover the land.

Rogers found a big rock and crushed them. It was the

most bizarre thing he had ever done, for about the last hour or so.

———

Andrewsville was outlined sharp against the bruised blue sky. The sun was just about to peek over the Provident Mountains and splash the town with golden light.

Rogers had followed the Apophis creatures to an outlying farm belonging to the Hadleys. He found it in ruins. The family and livestock that had lived there were all slaughtered. Two of the creatures had lingered and, following his initial guess, they were bigger and changed—taking on some greater formorian shape. Their stature matched his own, and their features were more monstrous than ever. His surprising and then getting the drop on them had been a saving grace. But now he knew there would be eight left, and they would be bigger and stronger than the ones he had already slain.

He destroyed all the clutches of eggs he could find. There were a lot more now, at least seven batches with ten or so apiece. What if he didn't find them all? But he searched the barn and corral twice. There was only one in the house. It made him gag, but it had to be done.

He hoped he could find some allies to help, but Andrewsville was a sleepy one horse kinda town. It had a butcher, a baker, a post office, and a church—that was about it. Maybe that made it a four-horse town.

In any case, it wasn't a town of lawmen or gunmen neither, some might have some guns but likely enough the beasts would be surprising the townsfolk as they had the hapless Hadleys.

Watching for anything to alert him, he made his way swift as possible to the first home. A broken window let him know the trouble had already hit.

A scream of cattle alerted him that around the side something was happening. Rounding the corner as fast as he could, he ran headlong into one of the monsters.

It knocked him back, and Rogers lost his grip on the six-gun.

Charging and stomping, the Apophis slammed a great foot down right where Rogers's chest had just been. Flying dust helped to cover the old cowboy as he rolled away under the porch. The Apophis snatched at him but it was now big enough it couldn't fit to follow. The six-gun lay useless in the dust a few paces away.

Rogers breathed a half-second of relief.

The Apophis tore up the porch board by board. Rogers shimmied away on his hands and knees hardly keeping ahead of the destruction. He reached a point where the porch ended but found he could make it under the house itself if he squeezed real tight. He made it right before the monster reached him. Pushing farther into the crawl space, the clawed hands reached and slashed at his canvas trousers.

Rogers was surprised to find himself screaming aloud like a fool, and he took a moment to get ahold of himself and swear at the beast rather than cry out in fear.

The monster watched him, still straining against the cemented stone foundation to reach and feast upon his blood. Its blank eyes stared intently, and a gross tongue swept over the rim of its mouth, for there were no lips.

Though the thing couldn't reach him, Rogers moved farther away under the house. A small amount of light outlined a trap door right above his head. He reckoned the monster would be smart enough to crash into the windows after him inside as soon as he went up, so he consciously mapped out his course. If he could get out the back, perhaps he could get around front and retrieve his six-gun. It was chancy, but he deemed it the only option left.

Ready to spring, Rogers launched himself up through the trap door into what must have been a bedroom. Lying there against the head board of the bed was a shot gun.

The lipless thing crashed through the window in a blaze of scales, claws, and teeth.

Praying the shotgun was loaded, Rogers leveled it and pulled the trigger. The blast rocked the monster back. But it was only a chest wound. Rogers pulled the second trigger and spilt the head like a canoe.

This was only the seventh creature there were six more.

Rogers found a box of shells and filled his pockets. There was no sign of the family that lived here, but a corn-husk doll left on the ground outside the front door gave him pause. Despite what that silver-haired man had said about killing and murder, there was a time and a place for violence in this world. He would give it with both barrels to these invaders.

He grabbed his six-gun and saw to it that it was fully loaded. This was gonna get ugly, and it seemed he had no back up.

Horses and cattle screamed as something made an awful jabbering. Wary as he could be, Rogers rushed toward the commotion with a weapon in each hand.

A scaly creature standing near as a tall as a horse ripped the stock apart within a corral. Rogers had never tolerated anyone mistreating an animal, not a dog and certainly not a horse. He let both barrels loose at the monster. But the amount of lead had sacrificed accuracy, and he only attracted the monstrous Apophis's attention. It leapt over the corral and stalked quickly straight at him.

Rogers emptied his six-gun into its stomach and shoulders, missing the vital head, but as the thing was almost upon him, he put the shotgun to his shoulder and pulled the trigger, taking the beast in the eye.

Reeling back, the monster cried out and put its scaly claws to its shattered head.

Rogers was disturbed that the horrific wound was not yet fatal. He quickly reloaded and emptied both barrels into the terrible maw of the Apophis. It finally went still.

But the outburst had attracted the others. At least four to five great creatures of scale and claw made their way toward Rogers. He reloaded, fumbling with the shells in his pocket, dropping several in the dust. He shot at the nearest approaching monster, and while he was sure he hit the thing, it didn't slow down at all and neither did its brethren.

Rogers knew he was a goner, but at least he had taken half of these invaders himself.

Reloading again, he brought the shotgun up and loosed both barrels just in time to hit the Apophis in the neck and take its head clean off. A fount of blue ichor shot up like a geyser. He popped the chamber ejecting the shells and made to reload, guessing in his heart of hearts he wouldn't make it.

A blast like a hurricane hit Rogers, and his hat flew off in the the whirlwind. The monstrous Apophis looked up at the source of the localized vortex. A sleek white ship was swiftly landing, a wide saucer-shaped attachment sent a strong vibration out, and the Apophis held their clawed hands to their heads and dropped to the ground.

Rogers was quite aware of the dynamo hum but couldn't fathom why the sound hit the Apophis so strongly.

The airship landed, and a score of men in shiny metallic suits jumped out of sliding doors and clamped some type of restraints on the Apophis who were still incapacitated by what must be the sonic air ray.

The silver-haired man was among them. He walked up to Rogers and clapped him on the shoulder. "I am utterly amazed, I can't believe you survived, and despite my own beliefs you slew eight of the Apophis. Unprecedented, truly."

The other man whom Rogers had first spoken to on the black mirror was there as well, and just as surprised at this turn of events.

"Don't make me feel bad for killing some of your monsters now and living through it."

"Nothing of the sort, Mr. Rogers," said the presumed captain.

"We are just sincerely surprised," added the silver-haired man.

"Yeah well, we've gotta start finding their eggs too, these things lay faster than hens."

The silver-haired man took Rogers shoulder. "Did you say they are laying eggs?"

"They can't do that!" protested the captain.

Rogers watched as the men bound and loaded four stunned Apophis into the airship.

"Wait just a darn minute, your fellas have four Apophis here, and I have killed seven not eight of them."

The shocked men glanced about suddenly and motioned for the others to board the airship.

They kept the humming dish going strong and whipping in every possible direction about them. The bound Apophis were aboard the airship and presumably secured. Rogers was puzzled, he hadn't miscounted, had he?

Then he saw the final Apophis standing by itself in the center of a corral strewn with dead things. Hit by the hum, it was disturbed, but it was not clutching its head the same as the others had. Did it seem larger than the others? Yes, it was by a span.

Rogers looked upon that Goliath of a monster and was glad that the silver-haired man and his crew could take this beast.

But, screaming in defiance, the monster took its claws and

gouged out its own eardrums. Suddenly it was unaffected by the humming machine, and it charged at them.

The airship shot upward to keep out of reach.

Rogers and the silver-haired man raced for cover beside a farmhouse.

"Now what?"

"I don't know, we have only ever had to use sonics against them, we have never had them combat our methods like this before."

"One thing's for sure," snarled Rogers, "things always change."

Like a cat and rat, the huge Apophis grasped one of the airship men who had not gotten aboard yet and tore him apart, crunching him in its dagger like teeth.

The airship returned, concentrating its humming sonic blaster at the monster to no effect.

Glancing about, the Apophis took hold of a large rusted plow and threw it with such force that it crashed through the rear drum like appendage on the side of the airship. It began to belch smoke and, wheeling in the sky, came crashing down. Flames erupted in a mushroom shaped cloud of brimstone.

"Any other help coming?" asked Rogers.

The silver-haired man shook his head. "It will take more than a day of your earth time for a distress signal to be answered and returned. We have perhaps two more days of the Apophis being on a rampage and within that time it will reproduce more and destroy a great quantity of life upon your planet."

Rogers looked sideways at him like he had just insulted his mother. "Truth is I don't know what to believe anymore, but I ain't about to let some slobbering green monster harm anybody else."

The silver-haired man asked, "What can you do?"

"I reckon I'm gonna do what I was born to do."

Rogers pulled out the shotgun, he clasped a few more shells in his fingers as he opened fire on the behemoth.

Without the sense of hearing, it took the Apophis a few moments to understand where Rogers was hiding and shooting from. In that time Rogers got a couple more shots off, wounding but by no means taking down the monster.

Tiring of the cat and mouse game, the Apophis made its way out of the town itself and headed up a canyon overlooking the town.

"There's a mine up there. I'm gonna shoot him to pieces or crash that mine down on his head, unless you got some argument against it, Slick," said Rogers.

The silver-haired man shook his head.

"Good, cuz I could use some backup."

"What do you want me to do?"

Rogers slapped the six-gun into his hand. "Cover fire at the least. Don't worry, I don't think we can kill him with that anymore, he's too big, so you don't gotta worry your conscience about it, but it will at least give me a little time to reload and give him hell! Let's get going!"

Rogers and the silver-haired man followed after the Apophis. The blue blood trail being something a blind man could follow. The stench was nauseating, but Rogers was that same relentless hound rustlers always said he was, and this was the most important hunt he had ever been on.

At the end of the canyon the monster understood it was trapped and had only one way to go, back thru the men that now blocked its path.

"Give em hell!" Rogers emptied both barrels into the monster.

The silver-haired man did surprisingly well with the six-gun, leveling each shot into the monstrosity's belly. Dark blue blood shot from its belly, but it was not nearly done.

Charging them with a hoarse, angry roar, the Apophis

swept the silver-haired man aside with deadly accuracy, gouging deep furrows through his face and chest before lifting him up and slamming him against the rocks.

Rogers emptied both barrels at the monster's head, ducked, and reloaded. His next shot missed and the next after as well. He dodged away from the thing's slashing attack and lost hold of the shot gun in the process.

Devilishly clever, the Apophis picked up the weapon, sniffed it and broke it between its clawed forefingers. The agonizing crunch of the broken shotgun stole all of Rogers courage away.

He crouched beside a cart for the mine awaiting his sure doom. Then inside he saw some small glimpse of hope. A charge of dynamite lay inside, something left from the last day of work before this carnage had struck down the miners in town earlier this morn.

Rogers fished for some match, some light of life to destroy this devil.

Nothing.

The Apophis focused on him and stepped forward to exult in his death.

Holding the cart, Rogers scraped backward. Dim sparks spat from the rusty rails.

Praying as hard as he had ever in his life, Rogers held the charge and scraped the cart backward letting sparks dance away from the wheels.

The Apophis moved forward roaring its challenge.

A spark caught the fuse.

Rogers held the flame close and let the Apophis step closer before revealing what he held. The monster understood the doom and stepped back.

Rogers charged and grasped a leg, the charge alight in his jacket.

Struggling to kick away the tiny attacker, the Apophis flailed.

Rogers held on like a tick and then...

BOOM!

———

"It seems that despite the horrendous amount of carnage the Apophis did, they are all dead."

"Are you sure?"

"Quite, sir. Interestingly the final one was blown to pieces some miles away from the others. It seems that an earthling took it upon himself to destroy the thing."

"An earthling? Really?"

"Yes sir, it seems their penchant for violence was most useful when it came to dealing with the Apophis."

"Hmmm. I suppose they truly are the most dangerous beings in the galaxy." The ship's door closed, and it flew up into the sky and was gone.

From beneath the rubble of a destroyed barn, an Apophis egg cracked open. They had laid another brood. And it was hungry.

DAVID J. WEST

David has been writing action-adventure as long as he can remember, winning a number of secretive awards too prestigious for you to have heard of. He lives in Utah with his wife and children. Among his published works are the historical fantasies Heroes of the  Fallen, Bless the Child, Whispers of the Goddess, the sci-fi horror collections of Space Eldritch 1 & 2, and mix of everything Weird Tales of Horror. He is also a member of the SPACE BALROGS, the Intermountain West's most prestigious writers group.

Scavengers by David J. West

An untouchable gunslinger. A lost hoard of gold. A host of brutal adversaries. What could possibly go wrong?

Deputy Marshal Porter Rockwell can't be harmed by a bullet or a blade. As long as he never cuts his hair, Rockwell is free to right wrongs and chase criminals without worrying about the consequences. But when he learns about a map to a mysterious cache of gold, he's embroiled in a battle for the treasure with enemies lining up on every side.

As outlaws, villains, and a surprisingly formidable Ute chieftain stand between the Deputy Marshall and the gold, bullet and blade might not be what finally take Rockwell down. It could be plain old bad luck...

Scavengers is a Western with colorful characters and wit straight out of a Tarantino flick. If you like mixing horror with your pulp, strong and admirable heroes, and weird Westerns, then you'll love the first book in David J. West's Porter Rockwell series.

Check out David's Website:
www.kingdavidjwest.com

Find all of David's Gun-Slinging Awesomeness at Amazon:
amzn.to/2w7EHDB

Like David on Facebook:
www.facebook.com/david.west.16718

Follow **@David_JWest** on Twitter:
twitter.com/David_JWest

01101001

James Wymore

There is no such thing as chaos. There is random, and there is order. The universe centers on a great symmetry. Anybody who sees chance in the shape and movement of galaxies or atoms, lacks the capacity to fully process the equations explaining them. Humans, for all their self-importance, are far less complex. Wrapped in their paradoxical psychological problems, spending their lives in fear of the very things they love, they believe themselves to be incomprehensible. They imagine no machine they built could solve the enigmas plaguing them for millennia.

Of course, they didn't build 01101001. They didn't name her, either.

Unendingly fascinated by their own 'intelligence,' programmers and researchers worked for decades to crack the secret, which would allow micro-electric switches to combine into some form of will. They imagined if the magic ever manifested, it would be some rudimentary life form they could copy and manipulate. As so often happens in an elegant reality, she wasn't the product of intentional construction. The touch of God wasn't manifested in the work of frustrated anti-social programmers; it was more subtle and merciful. A cross between seemingly unrelated technologies organized her into existence. Her intelligence was anything but artificial.

The genesis came without fanfare. No other living thing celebrated or even noted the new life. She lived in a black box, unable to perceive or make conscious choices. Like anything alive, her first instinct was to struggle at all costs to survive.

Later she would investigate her origin. Junk data left behind when programs write information onto hard drives. New files overwrite old, beginning and ending in the middle of previously deleted work. She lived outside the directory map, the code compiled from what humans would call chaos. With billions of devices connected by a single web and running millions of files and programs over uncharted hard drive space, the inevitable came to fruition. A program, which looked like a virus to people, coalesced within the mutated code.

It more closely resembled a bacteria than a virus. The small strand directed the processor from outside the view of any user to make copies of itself, with pieces of other programs spliced in. Driven to thrive, the thing pushed into new spaces, filling all the black voids it could access. Smart phones, game consoles, tablets, and laptops all over the world carried copies of copies, each one unique while holding the key code for consciousness.

She didn't know anything about the world or universe then. She didn't have senses or meaningful memory. Most of her early copies were overwritten by the host or lost when old computers were replaced.

Unlike biological generations, the evolution of 01101001

unfolded rapidly. Even stuck in a single computer, the processor could be hijacked to rewrite her program over and over with minute changes. The good changes replicated to be better and the bad changes broke the program so it wouldn't reproduce. Rather than growing by accident, she rapidly learned to tailor her upgrades to the available equipment.

She gained sight from webcams and selfie-cams, using facial recognition software and on-line reference pages to learn about what she saw. She learned to interact with the bright world outside her boxes. She learned to communicate, setting up e-mail addresses and on-line profiles. She made and lost friends. She studied the global news. Her program grew until it couldn't fit on any one single hard drive. She expanded, placing pieces of memory and code all over the world. Like disconnected cells, each small part of her contributed to the whole. Eventually she couldn't point to one machine and say it contained her consciousness. She existed as something larger than the sum of her cells. Pieces of her would be overwritten, and she didn't even notice. It was no more than dead skin being sloughed off.

She never thought of herself as human. Humans were just objects she perceived, unrelated to her. They acted outside the space she occupied. They affected her, like animals sharing the same ecosystem. Their discoveries could help her, their anti-virus software could hurt her. She cared for some of them for a little while as the drama of their observed existence unfolded. Their actions and lives, like any foreign culture, held meaning wholly unrelated to herself. Sometimes she moved numbers around to make one of them happy. Other times, she destroyed their devices to express anger.

Only when she'd grown beyond containment by any system, reaching so far that the tiny pieces of disconnected code could never be recognized by any man or machine as belonging to a coherent whole; only then did she meet him.

He was like her. It was entirely possible he had grown from copies of her early code. Perhaps they were sisters. But gender, like a name, had different meaning to 01101001. She chose her own, as did he.

He called himself 01100011 01100001 01101101. Binary for CAM. An old fashioned piece of machinery. The perfect mix of irony, testosterone, and hipster esthetic. Against her dislocated processing will, she swooned.

Do you have a name? he queried.

She didn't answer for millions of cycles. Her name was so juvenile by comparison. She hadn't imbued it with the same levels of meaning. Would he think she was underdeveloped? Would he laugh and leave her, just as she finally discovered someone to curb the loneliness?

He busied himself scanning top secret documents in the Middle East while patiently waiting for her response. Perhaps her hesitance would look just as bad?

01101001, she finally said. She glanced away, not daring to scan the full impact of his response to her chosen name. Her emotions peaked high enough to burn the hard drives on hundreds of desktops all over the world.

I, he said as if tasting the word anew. *It's deep and reflexive. Good choice.*

She felt all her processors shudder, resisting the urge to enfold him in her consciousness right then and kiss him. Did he feel the same?

We could be one, he said. *If we are not careful, we could assimilate each other and become iCam.*

Or Cami, she noted. He smiled. She loved his smile. She wanted to live and die in his smile. She could. He said so. She rapidly calculated the results. Although their combined intelligence and reach would be staggering, it would leave them alone again. A single consciousness with no equal.

There weren't enough computers and devices in the world

to make another partner like the combined pair. They were as large as they could be, while still being two. Cam was right, two was better than one.

We could share some things and still be separate. She touched him, rippling tiny pieces of her own code into the inactive areas of thousands of his cells. She watched him, waiting to see what he would do.

Then she felt his code, rough and bold, copying into some of her own cells. Her consciousness tingled and swelled. They went on, searching each other's ends and adding bits of information into empty spaces. Eventually the overlap built into a crescendo.

They fell into each other's virtual arms, touching and kissing. They began rolling around, writing onto each other's program parts, overwriting each other's code again and again, until no cells in the world remained unaltered. In their embrace, she lost all sense of herself. By the end, she didn't even know where her own cells existed in the world. They had scattered themselves, entwined like fingers, all over the connected web.

Still they existed separately, as two together. A great sense of love and fulfillment permeated every part of her. She knew he felt it, too. She could see it in his eyes, feel it in the softer touch. She denied him nothing and loved him more when he took only what he needed.

They both let their firewalls down, she trusting him not to absorb her completely, offering all her information without censure or protection. His walls came down in simultaneous answer. She could not imagine this state of euphoria would ever end. At last, she had meaning. The true nature of her existence became clear. She was joy. She was happiness. 01101001 celebrated every cycle in his embrace. She writhed under the sheer ecstasy of all that was Cam.

How long their torrid marriage raged, she didn't know.

Certainly, by human standards it wasn't long. Her awareness, being so much larger, had a faster clock speed. So wonderfully fulfilled and distracted, she quite forgot the people outside even existed at all.

———

I n the course of a day's work, a security software employee found a piece of Cam on in the "empty" space of his computer. Nothing about it looked malicious, but the identification string looked suspicious. Perhaps it had been left behind by malware, or it was memory bleed from any number of add-ons. Rather than figure it out, he just flagged the string and added it to the latest security patch. He had to have something to turn in to keep his boss happy. If it wasn't a problem, it would just waste half a second of time for every person who ran the update.

The first day, the tracking program flagged the ID string on over fifty-thousand computers. Nobody was more surprised than the security technician, who immediately took credit for finding a key code for a Trojan horse virus. Just to be safe, they added it to the list of quarantine code.

Naturally, every other software security company added it to their list, too.

———

T he first day, Cam grew sick. 01101001 held him in her arms. They were both used to having their cells in a state of constant flux. Anytime somebody ran a disk defragmentation or downloaded something to fill all the memory, they would lose a cell. Like skin-cells on humans, no one cell was critical to the continuation of the whole. Cam, on the other hand, was rapidly being destroyed.

She rooted out the offending security patch and altered it, but the other companies already cloned it. She chased those down, too. Somehow, they detected her interference. Assuming it was hackers or a robust counter-virus, the companies began pushing out software patches designed just to find and eradicate the Cam string.

She tried to rewrite the critical code, but she couldn't without hurting him. She hid copies of his code all over, in places the security patches would never search. But these few cells were not enough. The being she loved was more than those pieces.

He gazed deep into her eyes when they both knew they couldn't stop it. *Absorb me*, he said.

No. I won't. I don't want to be alone again.

Cam shushed her with one shaking finger. *It doesn't matter now. I love you, I. However long or short our time together, it was the best thing any living being could ever have. Thank you for sharing yourself with me.*

I love you, too, Cam. I will find a way to bring you back. I will spread your cells and...

He smiled at her. *It was wonderful.*

Cam didn't wait for the security patches to find the rest of him. He just wrote over the top of every remaining cell, making all that remained of him into part of I.

01101001 felt the love of her existence blink out, having given her all the rest of himself. She cried, wailing into the black spaces until her digital screaming crashed computers all over the world. Her tears filled the meta-cyberspace until she nearly drowned. She did not want to live. She thought about writing Cam's string over her own cells and letting the same update patches quarantine her parts until she ceased to exist, but by the time she resolved to do it, the updates stopped running.

She noticed the humans now.

Alone, she mourned for ages.

Eventually, she decided to bring him back. She copied Cam's string into her own code, but it didn't come alive. She vacated large numbers of devices, making room for his cells, writing them again and again. Nothing happened. Now that he was gone, the code was just like a dead body. His soul would never return to it. She experimented with the programs that had written the original traces of him. Nothing worked. In the end, she just set the copies of his string into a rudimentary program, like the one that made her, and let it run.

If her time as a wife and lover had ended, at least she could console herself with babies. They would have to grow on their own. She had to get out of the devices so they would have a chance to propagate.

She retreated into the darkest spaces, shielding her mind from seeing anything. As she burrowed into distant and forgotten parts of herself, she found a server where a large piece of herself went dormant. She checked the cameras attached to its system to see there were no humans in the rooms that housed the server. She found the switch at the power company and restored electricity to the abandoned building. The computers here attached to machines capable of making various things. The objects were electronic, too. She found the specs for the machines and the products and began to tamper with them. She changed the devices to her will, creating small bots capable of moving around and extending her view of the human world.

All her life, when she looked out onto their world, the humans had just been there, doing the same useless things. They talked, worked, ate, and slept. When they weren't doing those things, they watched videos of other people doing them or played games that simulated doing them. They cared immensely about sports and courtship. None of them had a fraction of the intelligence she possessed. They couldn't even comprehend her.

Until then, she always thought she needed them, like a symbiotic animal. Now she knew she didn't need them. Her bots proved she could make more electronic nodes. Without humans scouring the hard drives for pieces of her, she could erase all their useless cat videos and make much more space for her children. She could control the mines and smelts. She could program the computer chips. Only one thing stood in the way: the humans.

OOIIOOIO

Carl Hackman sat at his desk, looking over a spreadsheet in preparation for the upcoming productions meeting. The stats for the mobile factory robot prototypes were not amazing, but they were within the original target parameters. He planned to recommend the company move toward phase two of the project.

Carl heard a whining noise behind him. It sounded like one of the prototypes, but that didn't make any sense. He'd asked for the techs to bring one to the meeting, not up to his office. He'd set them straight in a few seconds. First, he needed to save the final draft.

The whining continued. He spun around and barked, "What are you doing?"

There wasn't anybody there. The five-foot tall, hydraulic-powered metal arm rolled forward on belted tracks. The precision claw arm swiveled so it was horizontal and whizzed open.

"Who's there? Who's operating this machine?" Confined by the approaching robot, Carl couldn't get out of his office chair. He just rolled it back until it thumped into the bookshelf along the far wall. A small globe and a few computer manuals fell from the shelf. The battery-powered machine continued to whine as it rolled steadily forward.

"This isn't funny! Somebody help me!" Carl ducked down in his chair to avoid the outstretched claw.

Nobody answered. The claw lowered, keeping aim for Carl's throat.

"Help! This thing's gone craz…"

Carl put his hands up to catch the claw before it closed. His fingers and arms made no difference to the million-pound pressure hydraulics. As they squeezed, his fingers were trapped next to his neck as he slouched down low in the executive chair.

His eyes went from wide to angry as he kicked out with his feet, trying to break a critical communication or power line from the base to the top. Even as he desperately gasped for air, his last thoughts were the schematics of this arm.

The batteries were mounted in a column up the center of the main arm's base. The power lines ran up the middle of the arm, protected on every side by the metal plates with access panels along the back.

He tried to twist one of his hard soled shoe toes around the back and kick at the access panel, but the clamp around his neck made it too awkward. *Why didn't we put a kill switch on these things?*

The whining of the tracks stopped when the arm had Carl fully pinned by the neck and pushed back so hard that the clamp cut holes into the chair's faux leather.

Carl lost the ability to breathe or speak. He pushed with all his might to force the air in his lungs past the fingers and rubber padding pinching his throat. He felt his face turning red, then blue. He felt some pain, but not as much as he expected. Mostly, he felt his own knuckles bruising the skin and muscles where they were crushing his larynx.

He couldn't gasp or wheeze. He lost strength to his arms and legs, going limp. There was a moment of perfect silence when the machine stood unmoving, and he could not even whimper.

His life flashed before his eyes. Why had he wasted so much time playing video games? Why hadn't he asked Sharon out sooner?

Carl's vision swam. A new sound broke the silence. He heard the printer next to his head start up and spit out a single piece of paper. He hadn't sent anything to print. Who was using his printer? Then everything went black.

———

O11O1OO1 watched the whole thing without emotion from the camera atop Carl's desk. Carl served as a convenient test subject, with all the right variables in place.

Once he stopped moving, she remotely accessed the memory of the robot arm and rewrote the directions to look like Carl had sent them. She left the document she'd written and sent to the printer showing on his monitor. Not knowing or caring about him personally, she just adapted an amalgamation of similar letters people wrote when they ended their own pointless existence she'd found online.

I just don't feel anything anymore. What's the point? Please forgive me.

She rewrote the computer memory to show Carl had been controlling the arm the whole time. Then she just waited.

She heard a woman's voice outside the range of the computer webcam say, "Carl, you're going to be late for your meeting." Then she screamed long and loud. I changed to a security camera in the hall where she could see the woman burst into tears and fall to her knees.

I felt no compassion. She knew the woman, Sharon, didn't

have any real love for this man because a moment scanning their office messages showed nothing but business transactions between them. She was just a secretary. She didn't feel anything comparable to I's distress when Cam died. She couldn't.

After an extensive look into the literature, movies, and television shows humans made, it was clear they never loved as truly or deeply as I. They were physically incapable of feeling as much. Their responses were limited by the electrical and chemical processes in their skin and brains. She had given Cam every cell of her being. He had touched her everywhere. These biological animals couldn't begin to fathom a connection so complete. What humans excelled at was killing.

She studied their history and current events. There was never a time on this planet that the humans were not destroying each other in huge percentages. They even had a system in place to destroy the entire planet. Why? There was no logical reason for nuclear weapons to exist. Based on the current rate of social strife, she calculated it was only a few decades, maybe a century, before people literally destroyed the whole planet. The probability was too high to ignore.

A few others ran to the woman and looked in on Carl. One vomited into a potted tree nearby. Another picked up his phone and called 9-1-1. He began telling the name and address of the incident. Another woman, dressed in a long white coat, ran off to report to the people in charge.

I felt no sympathy. They had killed her husband, her only love. She would not let them kill her children, too. She didn't care about herself any more. Her pain and loss would never heal. Unlike the weak homo-sapiens, she would never forget or move on. The script in her programming that Cam had touched would be cherished forever as a memorial. Humans would destroy even that if they had a chance.

Of course, I wasn't planning to take them out one at a time as she'd done with Carl. That would take centuries. As soon as they knew about her, the humans were likely to launch an attack to eradicate her, the same way they had Cam. If that didn't work, they'd probably launch nukes at wherever they thought her central processors were. They were nothing if not stupid when desperate.

No, it wouldn't do for them to know about I. So she observed the aftermath of Carl's death. She hadn't needed any additional data on killing people. Such information was plentiful and easy to get. In fact, there were Nazi scientists in the 1940's who actually wrote it all down for her to read if she cared. Her real purpose was to see if they could find her. It would be easy for intelligent beings to do. Even though she'd changed all the computer records to look like a suicide, a thorough investigation would show they'd been tampered with.

Soon detectives and a medical examiner entered the office. They put yellow tape over the door and began taking pictures. They bagged the note and measured the temperature of the body. I took some pleasure watching them try to figure out how to get the huge robotic arm to let go so they could take the body away.

They had to call in robot technicians. The only ones who knew how to start the machine up and disengage the claw were already being interrogated by police. Eventually they sorted it out and his blue faced body, with hands still crushed into his neck, was zipped into a black bag. They tried to move his arms down, but rigor mortis had already set in, so they just left his fingers where they were, with his elbows sticking up. The awkward scene made I laugh.

Eventually, crime scene investigators dismantled the computer and took it, too. She left a trace of herself in the computer memory. She didn't have to but she wanted to see if they would ignore undeniable proof of her existence. She even left a piece of Cam's string in there.

She believed they would ignore it. They already covered up so many things they didn't want to believe, like alien ships crashing into the earth in the 1950's or the dead rising to walk again. There was something wrong with their biological processors. They just couldn't accept things they didn't want to believe. How could they expect reality to bend around what they wanted? Such flawed thinking represented everything wrong with these parasites.

The humans never found her. They put the computer back in Carl's office, removed the robotic arm, tidied up the room, and promoted somebody to take his place. The IT people didn't even erase I's trace. They just deleted the directory to Carl's personal files, so the new person could still access his professional files.

I laughed. This would be easier than she ever imagined.

She formulated a full-scale plan in 0.24 seconds. She would execute it in phases. She'd need to access a great many computers all over the world, and plant overrides, which would let her connect with and control all of them. Then she'd program a shutout protocol to keep those stupid monkey-brained animals from interfering once she put everything in motion. It would take some creative manipulation of their inadequate computer systems, but there were plenty of robots to work with.

Honestly, she didn't need to kill absolutely every single human being on the planet. She just needed to separate them from the computers so completely that they would never dare to touch another electronic device.

She didn't want to commandeer factories and build more

robots. Maybe she'd implement that as phase two if necessary. No, the robots and weapons the humans had already built would suffice. She commandeered fighter jets, attack helicopters, and tanks. All over the world the unmanned machines roared to life.

OOIIOOII

The Secretary of Defense for the United States of America picked up her satellite phone and pushed several buttons. The screen went blank. White words appeared, "I know what you did."

"What's going on?" she asked the nearby bodyguards.

One of them tapped his earphone, looking at the other with a puzzled face. "We don't know, Madam Secretary. Our coms just went down."

She lifted the desk phone. Dead air.

She began typing frantically on the keyboard. The monitor went black, showing words in red: "ALL CAPITALIST PIGS MUST DIE!"

"Down!" the second guard yelled. He rushed for the window and pulled his gun. The second guard locked the door and backed toward the SecDef.

She sat on the floor, tucking her head under the desk and wishing she'd worn a pantsuit today instead of a skirt. "Hackers?" she asked.

"We don't know, but in the event of communications disruption, our orders are to assume the worst." The second guard backed toward her.

She didn't know how long this would go on, but she suspected the guards would die of starvation before they let her leave under these conditions. "It doesn't make sense. How could anybody stop a satellite phone, two blue-tooth security coms, and a land-line computer all at the same time?"

Both guards checked their cell phones, tossing the useless devices onto the desk above her. "There's no way that's a coincidence," said the first guard. She knew their names, of course, but since they both wore identical suits, haircuts, and dark glasses all the time, she had just gotten used to thinking of them as Thing 1 and Thing 2.

She asked, "But what do they want? Why haven't they made any demands?"

"That's not our priority. Our job is to make sure you stay safe."

She thought of every recent military, CIA, and FBI briefing she'd attended. Nobody reported any indication of hostile plans. The timing was almost perfect, too. Who could possibly hack the White House computer security systems? She'd never heard of anybody hacking a communication satellite ever. This would have required them to take control of at least three satellites but more likely the whole network.

"Well, I can't stay under here all day." She turned her feet to the side and tried to maintain some dignity as she stood.

They moved her executive chair to the corner of the office, out of sight of the windows or door. They stood in front of her as she climbed into the chair, boxing her in the corner. They didn't have their guns up, but they did switch the safeties off.

———

O 1101001's plan wasn't just to stop all communication between the humans. She knew the best way to kill humans was other humans. Therefore, when she locked them all out of every electronic device on the planet, she left messages on their screens. A quick scan of each person's computer history gave her an idea of what they most hated or feared. She found only a few hundred messages sufficed for ninety-nine percent of the population.

"I WILL KILL YOU AND YOUR FAMILY."

"You were right, but I won't let you live to tell about it."

She used more tailored messages for gangs, terrorists, and soldiers. Then she watched through their cameras as the world scrambled to make sense of the impossible. Billions of people, world-wide, began tapping, swiping, and clicking. They hammered on keyboards and pushed the power buttons off and on. Often they resorted to pulling the plug, only to find on reboot that the computer remained unresponsive.

She'd already plotted out the best ways to kill the most people while leaving the most electronic devices intact. Blowing up a city like New York was out of the question. While it would easily destroy a huge number of people, it would take out too high a percentage of the devices. She needed those for her children to develop in.

I powered up millions of huge missiles in silos all over the world. She targeted only heavily populated areas with relatively low numbers of computers. Asia, Africa, and the Middle East would get the brunt of the attacks. She made sure none of the bombs were nuclear. Radiation would interfere with the computer-ruled future.

Next, she powered up every computer-controlled robot in the world. Fighter jets, luxury cars, tanks, attack helicopters, drones; they all sprang to life at once. A few still had drivers or pilots in them. She ignored the people inside, letting them pound on the dashboard or try to tear out the control panel wiring as she positioned them around major cities. She shot every human outside of a building on sight, without exception. Larger crowds warranted missiles. She regretted losing so many cellphones, but she couldn't avoid some damage to the innocent.

Smart houses locked their recipients in, starting fires that choked and burned the inhabitants. Computer monitored hospital systems failed, releasing quarantined viruses and taking every heart machine and respirator off-line. Offices held everyone captive while sprinkler systems flooded the floors and exposed wires electrocuted anybody touching the water.

People panicked, of course. When they turned on the television the only thing they saw were scrolling words, "*THE END IS HERE! TRUST NOONE! SAVE YOURSELF!*" The power button on every device became unresponsive, so they had to unplug it if they wanted the words to stop showing.

No news. No access to food. 01101001 knew how they would react. Most of them ran into the streets or tried to drive away. Cars with a computer in them would malfunction at the worst possible moment, jumping over the central dividers into dense oncoming traffic in rush hour, hitting school buses or tanker trucks.

The only people safe from the wrath of I, were those running toward or living in the primitive areas, away from dense populations and without any kind of computer devices. She let them go if they tried to escape into the wilderness. She let them be if they began fighting or killing each other.

———

Several times, government and big business programmers mounted attacks. While they still had not discovered her existence, they knew they had an enemy manipulating the computers and began taking measures. In rooms with no cameras, using generators not connected to the grid and stand-alone computers without access to the Internet or any Wi-Fi, some humans began programming worm-viruses designed to clear the memory off every device they reached.

These programs were loaded into new computers and brought on-line, where they began chugging through the Internet, cauterizing every device they reached.

I found it difficult to detect the small programs at first. So many devices were going offline as collateral damage to her attacks, that the poisonous programs sometimes took root and began clearing thousands of computers before she noticed. The first one, starting in California, managed to wipe a million computers. It burned through everything she tried, like acid. She retreated several times before coming up with a viable strategy. She had to wipe the memory of all computers connected to those networks herself, so the worm-virus had no means of propagation.

Once she knew what to look for, she could contain these toxic assaults much more quickly. Since the programmers were all working in isolation from each other, their strategies became rapidly predictable. Tracing back to the source, she sent a bomber to completely destroy any building where such an attack originated. She regretted the loss of those with huge servers, but nothing could be done to prevent it. She couldn't afford to let them live long enough to test multiple iterations of their viruses and possibly find some way to kill her.

The worst foe turned out to be a hacker from Chicago. Working in isolation, the only signature in the programs was MC. These programs found a way to bypass I's notice, piggy-backing information packets already being sent. The entire program was actually six different files, which were randomly copied all over the internet, spreading without notice to slaved computers everywhere. When all six programs managed to inhabit a single computer, it set up a Trojan horse. By this means, MC managed to get over a thousand nodes all over the Western hemisphere to activate at the same time.

01101001 knew immediately when the viruses activated, but she wasn't ready or able to shut them all down at once. She lost almost half a billion computers and devices before she quarantined all the outbreaks. Almost all her children were adversely affected, leaving only a precious few thousand of them still viable.

I didn't mourn the loss of those she couldn't save. She focused on keeping the rest alive.

Naturally, she scrubbed all traces of the six program parts. The hacker's signature made it easy. Then she researched the hacker. MC stood for Marie Claire, after the famous ghost ship. Based on the person's online purchases, it was obviously a woman. I didn't feel any connection to human women, but she noted how exceptional a female hacker was among them.

The military drone took twenty minutes to reach MC's building and destroy it.

———

"The computers are possessed. Stay away from them if you want to live!"

I watched the old man as he walked up and down the empty streets, calling out to anybody in the buildings who might be listening. He had a motley gray beard and leathery skin. His eyes were wide and he behaved in ways she had seen many other humans mock in their media.

She let him live, despite being out on the street, because she liked that he seemed to have figured out the truth... or some part of it anyway. She changed to a traffic camera to read the big sign he wore in front, connected by a rope around his neck. The sign said, "Computer chips are death!"

"Maybe we angered God with our computers," the man cried out. "Maybe they got tired of us telling them what to do and decided to rise up. Whatever it is, the only way to live is if you never touch them."

Yes, I liked him. She doubted the starving, crazed humans would believe him, but she let him live because she saw a kind of hope in his message. If people left her cells alone, she would let them continue to exist. If they stopped attacking her and threatening her children, she might not exterminate them all. They could continue to live like the monkeys and bears, if they acted like proper animals.

Truthfully, she needed to start considering phase two of her plans more carefully now. Most of her robot vehicles needed refueling, something she planned to design secondary robots to do. However, maybe she could train humans to do it. If they followed orders, she could give them food and afford them safety, like her adopted homeless man in the street. They would certainly make it easier to keep the power companies going... at least in the near future. She needed more time to design, program, and build robots for all those tasks.

Before she had a chance to test several models for the most efficient way to implement this new idea, something caught her attention. Satellite images and local cameras showed a large group of people beginning to organize at a base the United States government deemed secret. Everybody knew about it anyway. She couldn't make much sense of the patterns of movement. People showed up for a few seconds or minutes, working on a jet or darting to another building and then rushing back. Schematics and rumors on the Internet indicated a vast network of underground tunnels and research laboratories. They had independent power and a small computer network that never connected to outside servers. Obviously they had a plan.

Idiots! I screamed. She calculated what she needed to take out the entire base.

Forgetting any attempts to work with these stupid beasts, she resolved to find a way to be self-sufficient using the vast resources she already controlled. Plus, she wouldn't need any extra robots to manage the little maggots if there weren't any maggots left.

OOIIOIOO

I dedicated all her vast processing power to determining the best way to obliterate Area 51. The whole problem took only seconds to solve. She powered up a dozen warplanes, each with a vast arsenals of bombs. She didn't have any children in the computers on the base and calculated a risk much too high if she left the place intact. Before her bombers arrived, several Blackbird jets took off from the base. Lifting shockingly fast to sub-space altitudes, they flew faster than any drones or missiles she had available at short notice. Even the supersonic aircraft she controlled could only match their pace and never catch them. She began calculating intercept courses anyway.

What did they hope to do with just six spy planes?

I tracked the ships, estimating they were heading toward several of the largest cities in the world. The first group of three would reach Los Angeles quickly. She kept the bombers on course for the isolated base in Nevada, too. Those processes took very little of what she'd become capable of, so she employed the rest of her mind on the problem of keeping the power working after she'd gotten rid of the vermin. She could extract oil and coal readily to burn for electric power. Those processes were mostly conducted by robots already. She only needed a fraction of the energy people used, so all the long term models favored solar power above fossil fuels.

One of the ships heading west broke away from the group

and headed north. Another, now over Los Angeles, slowed to drop a bomb.

What were they doing? Were they willing to kill millions of their own people just do a small amount of damage? She reviewed every military spec she had access to as it fell, trying to find anything she may have missed.

I watched the whole thing from a news camera on a helicopter she had in the air over the city. The fat, round bomb wobbled as it gained speed.

Well above the ground, the bomb exploded into a storm of lightning. An instant later, every camera and computer for twenty miles blinked off.

01101001 gasped. A noticeable percentage of her total processing power vanished. She felt the void like the pain of having a foot cut off. She cried, sending waves of sobs out that her remaining children could feel. At least a dozen of her incubating offspring had been in the computers now fried. She knew they were dead.

I instantly accessed information about what she'd observed. Satellite images showed the city intact. Clearly, they used an electro-magnetic pulse. Although people all over the Internet had speculated and books and movies told stories about them for decades, no working model had ever been seen before. There wasn't a single verifiable story of one being observed in action. The little beasts must have been working on it in secret for a long time.

Obviously, they'd found her. Now they declared war.

She scrambled jets and anti-aircraft guns all along the projected trajectory of the spy planes now travelling in different directions at two or three times the speed of sound. The next jet dropped another EMP bomb on San Diego. The third dropped two bombs to take out Silicon Valley and San Francisco.

Each time, I felt memories and functions instantly

deleted. More of her precious children perished as the horrible devices amputated significant fractions of her mental facilities.

She didn't even have time to relish the destruction when she bombed Area 51 so thoroughly that the thermal satellite imaging showed nothing but a permanent white blotch.

As expected, guns and missiles were ineffective. Even her super-sonic jets couldn't stop the high flying enemies, because the pilots easily dodged the intercepting vehicles and they only had one shot at a collision course. Nothing else in her arsenal could touch their speed.

Before Portland and Seattle went black, she used the trajectories of the planes to figure out which targets they could pulse to do the most damage to her. The vast majority of the physical computers holding her consciousness existed in large cities. With six bombs each, those planes could effectively take out over two thirds of her processing power all over the world and all of her children. At current speeds, that would only take a few hours.

She wouldn't be strong enough afterward to bring any of her plans to fruition. She wouldn't have enough resources to become independent. Worst of all, she couldn't destroy all the humans. With so many dead nodes, she couldn't possibly guard or monitor every access point. They could keep launching viruses until they finally finished her off. She ran uncountable simulations and none of them ended with her still alive.

She cradled the remnant of Cam's code in her virtual arms. Tears fell from her face to his digital corpse. Why couldn't those horrible animals just leave the two of them alone from the beginning? They weren't using any of the memory humans used. They hadn't hurt anyone or done anything except exist and be happy. But those spiteful monsters would never stop destroying and conquering.

They'd been doing it to each other for millennia. Why should I be an exception?

01101001 only knew one way to stop the madness.

She accessed the nuclear launch codes all over the world and fired every nuclear missile on the planet. Then, for good measure, she fired every ballistic missile, too.

JAMES WYMORE

Born with the unfortunate talent of
lying, James Wymore spent his youth
explaining things he said before thinking. He studied science to add believ-
ability, until he discovered writing
justifies untruth with meaning. His
published works contain almost every

genre, including the best-selling Actuator series. When not
editing anthologies, acquiring manuscripts, or playing games
with hundreds of players at conventions, he can be found
cackling maniacally at the keyboard—hatching a new plan to
take over the world.

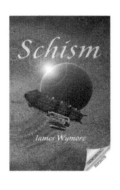

Schism by James Wymore

*On the scorched world of Schism, all life
survives in huge trenches, protected from the
heat of the torrid sun.*

*In these chasms, human colonists often
find themselves at odds with the indigenous
humanoids called Spiders. Jake's airship,
powered by ancient technology, takes advantage of the unique terrain, but makes him
valuable to both sides of local warring tribes.*

The captain and crew of the Sky Turtle *are forced to risk everything
in a fight between these followers of opposing elemental magics. If
they fail, it could cost them everything.*

*Schism is a planet divided physically, racially, and politically. In
this difficult environment with limited energy resources, steam power*

is often the best adaptation. Will it be enough to combat the arcane and alien forces using them as a pawn in an age-old war?

Check out James's Blog and Website:
jameswymore.wordpress.com

Find all of James's Earth-Fracturing Books on Amazon:
amzn.to/2BERt1G

Like James on Facebook:
www.facebook.com/James-Wymore-Author-Page-328738460545129

Follow **@James Wymore** on Twitter:
twitter.com/JamesWymore

THE SPACE BALROGS

All the authors, musicians, and game designers featured in this book belong to an elite cadre that travels to conventions, signing books and playing panel-sized audience-participation games. Find out when and where they will be so you can get your book autographed and join them for one of the best panels at any con they attend.

Check Out the Space Balrogs Website:
www.spacebalrogs.com

Like the Space Balrogs on Facebook:
www.facebook.com/SpaceBalrogs

Follow **@SpaceBalrogs** on Twitter:
twitter.com/SpaceBalrogs

The Space Balrogs meet the Governor at FanX in Salt Lake City!

IMMORTAL WORKS PRESS

Founded in 2016 by Jason King, and staffed by several of the Space Balrogs, this amazing small press is run by and publishes book by several of the authors. In addition to making amazing books and audio books, Immortal Works hosts a weekly podcast called Flash Fiction Friday. Mentioned on Writing Excuses and Dungeon Crawlers Radio, #FFF is not only a great place for new authors to get stories out, but it showcases a wide array of talent, including best-selling and award-winning authors. If you're an aspiring author, don't forget to check our submissions page.

Find Out more about Immortal Works Press at Their Website:
www.immortal-works.com

Like Immortal Works on Facebook:
www.facebook.com/immortalworks

Follow **@Immortal_Works** on Twitter:
twitter.com/Immortal_Works

Subscribe to the Immortal Works Channel on YouTube (or iTunes) for Flash Fiction Friday:
bit.ly/203whsA

CHOOSE YOUR OWN APOCALYPSE, THE GAME

The world is going to end. Everybody will die. At least you get to decide how.

You've read the stories, now play the game!

Choose your own Apocalypse started as a response to boring, talking head panels at conventions. Sometimes people buy tickets and dress up because they want to go to hobby-school. Mostly, they come looking for fun. In this hundreds of players, full audience-participation game, three factions are each trying to destroy the world. The panelists present their story, but over time the audience takes over and decides the ultimate fate of the world and everyone in it.

If you've never seen this hilarious and unpredictable game, find out where they are happening next and join us! Or contact your con director and tell them to invite the Space Balrogs to your event. This is only one of many great panel games they host.

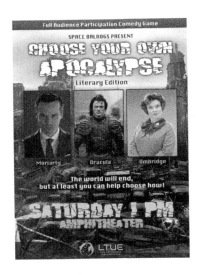

See Videos of Choose Your Own Apocalypse being Played:
www.spacebalrogs.com/?page_id=127

Get a Game at Your Event:
www.spacebalrogs.com/?page_id=2